ALSO BY MIKE PLAYER

<u>Non-Fiction</u>

Out On The Edge: America's Rebel Comics

<u>Fiction</u>

Viral

Hyperloop To Hell

www.MikePlayer.net

(Sign up for Mike's newsletter)

For Joel

Utopia

Mike Player

1. THE ADVENTURE SPOT

May 15, 1856

There was no place better to be. Christian Joseph St. Martin fidgeted. The thirteen-year-old's eyes widened with excitement as he finished another chapter of *The Horrifying Deeds of Stagecoach Bertha*.

He looked up from his perch. The low-cut post at the train platform warmed by the sun offered the best vantage point. If for only a few moments, the constant sour ache of boredom and loneliness drained away. His book bag strained with western penny-novels forbidden by his religious parents.

The 10:17 from Cleveland appeared in the distance. The engine chugged. Beneath the blue spring sky, black smoke dusted the horizon.

He shoved his book inside the satchel and pushed his glasses higher up on the bridge of his nose. He jumped down off the post, brushed off the back of his breeches, and grabbed his jacket to hurry over to the center of the platform. Several men and women joined him to wait.

To calm his racing heart, the boy took deep drafts of the cool Ohio air. He felt grateful to be away from his father's sick room back at the house and all the hovering Presbyterian dullards.

The train rumbled into the station. The engine gasped as it came to a squealing stop.

A sea of passengers and people there to meet them engulfed the boy. Impressions and colors washed over him; women's scarlet hats and men's brown jackets, workmen, black soot, acrid cigar smoke, mothers with small children dressed in red bows and traveling clothes, blue luggage and dark green trunks, porters and carriages waiting beyond the office, wagons and the smell of horses. The boy became intoxicated, and his focus sharpened.

Travelers from the eastern cities – businessmen, Mormons, poor immigrants. He wasn't looking for the usual person.

The boy lingered, the last one on the platform. Letdown always grew strong after the train emptied, like when Christmas was over. He sighed.

Before he turned to go, he noticed from the last car two persons stepping gingerly off the train. The boy had not seen black and white striped pants before! The blue of the taller man's coat practically shone in the sunlight, and a glint came from what looked like brass buttons. Long black hair hung down to the man's shoulders. He was handsome in an odd way. His face wasn't angular yet he was skinny around the middle. He commanded attention. The shorter man in the plain brown jacket was Black and wore a tall hat, a beard, and carried an orange duffel bag. He walked with a strange swagger.

Christian Joseph hurried down the length of the platform in order that he might introduce himself. *When you find your heart's desire,* thought the boy, *the long months of hopelessness and despair disappeared.* Everything was meant to be.

He rushed up to the long-haired man in the striped pants holding the cargo bag. "Mister! Can I carry your luggage?"

"At last, someone with manners in this godforsaken frontier," came a strong voice. "I worry you don't look fit enough to carry all of our things."

"Not fit enough!" Christian Joseph drew himself up. "I may wear glasses, but I once dragged our sick cow across a field by her hind legs all by myself."

"You can carry my bag," the smaller man said. "I'm a doctor. Do you work for one of the hotels?"

"Me? Oh, no. This platform is my Adventure Spot. I'm a minister's son."

"Well, we won't hold that against you," the man with the striped pants said. They began walking toward the gate to the street. The boy's balance grew lopsided from carrying the weight of the doctor's bag.

"Do you need a place to stay?" Christian Joseph asked. "My papa's dying, but we have a room we rent, cheaper than any hotel you'll find. And we might want another doctor."

"My God, boy, your papa's dying? Why in the world are you here when you should be with him?" asked Striped-Pants.

"He won't notice," Christian Joseph answered. "My father's been dying for two weeks. He's got the whole church congregation bringing him beans and broth and praying and singing. I can't even get close to him. His bed has become an altar."

The doctor leaned in close to the other man and whispered, "Maybe we should. No one would think to look for you there."

There was something not quite right about the doctor, thought the boy. "Are you in show business?" Christian Joseph asked as he pushed open the gilt iron gate and they stepped out onto the wooden planks of the street walk.

"You might say so," the taller man said. "Aren't we all made-up people? We'll need your room for the night. We are leaving in the morning for St. Joseph. I am Andrew Bolding."

The boy turned his bright face up to Andrew. "I am Christian Joseph St. Martin." *What were colorful-dressing men like these called? Fops?* The eyes of the taller man even appeared outlined in black pencil. "You're like one of the characters in my western novels. I bet you've got a gun!"

"Mind your business," the foppish man said. "What I've got are bruises, and here now what is this?"

A young muscular dockworker with a bare chest strutted past the little entourage on his way to the lakeshore.

"Down boy," the doctor told Andrew, and to Christian the doctor whispered, "Have you seen anyone suspicious, big and scary, waiting here for the train? Maybe looking in all the windows searching for someone?"

Christian thought earnestly a moment. "No. But I wish I had!" The boy thought his new friends were funny and different, and he couldn't wait to bring them home and show them to his papa.

The only relief from anxiety came from action, yet this time, Goiter was woefully under-prepared. He trudged along Fourth Street, his hands shoved deep inside his pockets. He had no bag, no extra clothing, nothing that would prepare him for riding trains and God knew what else farther and farther toward the frontier. He had never been farther west than New Jersey, and that was just to murder a newspaper art critic.

He walked several blocks until the street turned south and large houses began to line the walkway. Along a thick row of hedges he stopped and flung himself down to sit cross-legged on a clean stretch of planking, out of sight of the ten or twenty other pedestrians out and about, and the few wagons and carriages clattering past.

Everything pointed to disaster and toil without reward. Not to mention, Goiter's ten dollars had dwindled down to just three. He'd have to rob someone again soon. His old black coat showed holes at the elbows. His clunky black shoes wouldn't last much longer. His blue cloth cap made his face look bigger than it was.

He wanted a bath, and he wanted a woman, and he wanted some peace from the constant chatter inside his head. Murdering was hard. You had to worry about getting caught. Plus, you had to prevent getting killed yourself. Victims frequently fought for their lives. Then there were the rules of the gang. Murders had to be covered up and bodies disposed of properly.

He thought of his dead brother. "Gang life won't kill *me*," Goiter muttered.

There was no one to look after him, not even on the rainy evening long ago on the immigrant boat from Prussia, when he found his father seated atop the top deck railing, about to throw himself into the sea. Rain had pelted Goiter's face as he ran toward the elder Potts.

"Don't come any closer!" his father had shouted.

There had been no one else on deck. They were aft and behind one of the covered lifeboats.

"Don't do it!" Goiter pleaded. "Don't do it, father!"

"Goiter," his father said, a softness in his voice and a sadness in his eyes. "I am sick. You don't want me with you in America. It is better this way. For everyone."

"But–"

"Life is nothing, son. It moves too quickly, and it hurts too much. Death is a blessing. You'll make me proud. I'm sure of it. Take care of your brother."

Goiter took a step closer. His father pushed off from the railing.

Goiter gasped and peered over the edge. The black waters churned vast and empty.

Death was everyday and nothing special; if anything, death ended problems once and for all.

And Goiter learned later, you could make a living at it.

All the muscles in his body tensed. Across the street walking south he spied a bookish schoolboy leading a willowy bearded Black man and a brightly dressed fop with long black hair wearing striped pants. They took no notice of Goiter as Goiter was obscured by hedges, but he could see them well enough to positively identify the fop he was hired to murder.

I am smart! thought Goiter. *I did the right thing. I'm here at the right time, and I've found the fop.* Goiter didn't know how to dress snappy like the fop. Goiter's brown hair could never be jet-black and combed right. Goiter didn't know how to carry himself with panache.

But, he had tracked his prey!

His impulse was to bolt right up and run across the street, shoot the fop with his Colt .45 and run away. But, Goiter knew better. He would follow the little party and wait for the right moment to kill.

2. Grim Within

Andrew always got claustrophobia when surrounded by Protestants.

He and the doctor waited in the stuffy foyer for Christian Joseph St. Martin to inform the gathering at his home he had found help. A wave of condescension and disdain was sure to follow. Andrew inspected his black painted nails. They signified something, something his father would never allow, something no one even in New York would approve of.

No air circulated through the closed windows of the house. Everyone inside wore starched collars except the dying father who lay flat on his back. Dim light filled the halls whilst white glare streamed through the windowpanes. The father rested on an enormous couch in a nest of starched white pillows surrounded by clean towels and women showing deathly worried faces.

"Christian!" A woman sporting a drab beige waistcoat and a sad wool skirt exclaimed and practically flew down a huge staircase at the boy. The woman's face looked scrubbed clean and almost gray. She might have been pretty once.

When she at last held the boy close and allowed herself to give them her full attention, Christian said, "Mother, I have some renters for our spare room. They just got off the train."

She appeared as if she had taken a bite from a sour egg. "I'm sorry," the mother said. "We have no room to rent here."

"Yes, we do, Mother," Christian Joseph St. Martin said. "I was playing in it this morning, remember? You were crying and you slapped the maid? You said you were going to lose the house once daddy was dead because of all the money he owed and –"

The mother clapped a hand over Christian's open mouth. The boy struggled briefly and then stopped still and appeared very angry. "I said no such thing. Our boy reads too many of the wrong books," and to Christian she said, "Your father is just behind us, darling!"

"I could see to him. I'm Dr. Gray from New York Hospital."

There were some snickers from the shadows of the room. "A doctor?" the mother asked with disbelief. Her demeanor softened noticeably. "Our church doctor told us there was nothing left that we could do."

Dr. Gray set his orange bag on a handsome maple end table. "What is the problem?"

"My husband fell off of the roof. He broke his legs, and he's not right inside."

"May I see him?"

The mother did not move aside. "He detests inverts and Blacks."

"I am not an invert," Dr. Gray said.

"No?" The mother glanced at Andrew.

"Madame," Andrew said. "I am a traveling showman. I do impressions of Gainsborough's *The Blue Boy* for wealthy art connoisseurs."

Dr. Gray shoved an elbow into Andrew's side.

"Wasn't the Blue Boy an invert?" The mother's eyes narrowed.

"Let me in." Dr. Gray edged his way around the woman and her angry son and met no resistance.

Doilies were everywhere, under lamps and brass crosses and cups of water.

Two men in church clothes stood nearby. Andrew noticed one of them was heart-wrenchingly handsome and hardly twenty. "Deacons," the mother explained. And close to them sat two young women both drab like the mother. Christian Joseph St. Martin was the only child.

The couch supporting the father stood on clawed lions' feet.

"I'm a doctor," Dr. Gray told the gasping man.

The man looked to be barely forty. His eyes opened, and there showed only pain and annoyance. "I must have already died. A Black doctor! Does he have his papers?"

"I am a free man passing through from the north." The doctor removed his stethoscope and began a basic examination.

"Christian Martin, come away from that...man," wheezed the father when his gaze fixed on Andrew.

Christian Joseph St. Martin looked up at Andrew and then back at his father before taking two steps to his left toward the wall.

"The church doctor is a quack," the gasping father told the doctor. "He had me waiting all night before –" And then the minister labored under a wracking cough which brought up blood.

Dr. Gray's expression turned somber. "You've bled inside. I can give you something for the pain."

The mother approached the bedside. "That's more than our church doctor could do. He was out of morphine because I think he used it all up himself. He went to go get more yesterday, and we haven't heard from him since."

The doctor administered the morphine and the dying man's eyes slowly closed.

Several of the church people put their arms around the mother and led her to a room off from the staircase. "Christian Joseph, show these men to the empty room. They can stay there tonight – no charge."

"Thank you, ma'am," Andrew said from the front foyer.

She didn't look at Andrew, but she nodded once at the doctor.

"Come with me!" Christian Joseph said, and he led them through a whitewashed hallway and out the back door.

The room was a cabin in the back "where the slaves used to live."

Dr. Gray appeared to shrink into himself. Andrew linked his arm with the doctor's.

"What happened to the slaves?" Andrew asked.

"We had to sell them all to pay papa's creditors," Christian Joseph St. Martin said. "But that's not the real reason."

He opened the cabin door, and Andrew found the interior to be clean enough. A large feather bed with a blanket sat inside over a neatly swept wood floor. No glass filled the windows.

Books covered the floor. Some lay open as if their reading had been interrupted.

"This is where I come to read. Mama won't come out here. Not any more least ways."

"Maybe all the white people should sleep in one. There must be twenty books in here, boy."

Titles strewn about the floor that Andrew could read, included: *Firebrand the Mountain Man, Queer Frontier,* and *Shootings, Scalpings, and Sin!*

"You're like the men in my story books," Christian said, when they had closed the door behind them and all stood in the cabin.

"You keep your eyes open," Andrew warned. "There's a big brown-haired man in a tattered jacket following us. If you see him anywhere near your house, you tell me right away. We're all in danger."

Christian Joseph St. Martin became positively entranced.

"Which we are about to remedy right this very instant," Andrew added. "Doctor, I'm going to teach you how to shoot."

"You know how I feel about that."

"I need your help. Do you think the brunette monster is the only assassin they sent after me?"

Andrew asked the boy where they could target shoot.

"I was in the war," Dr. Gray's voice contained an edge. "...with Mexico."

"Close your mouth, boy," Andrew told Christian, and then to the doctor, he said, "But never fired your weapon. I know the man that has been sent to kill me."

"What man?" cried Christian Joseph in ecstasy.

"Never you mind," Andrew said.

"I know a place where you can target shoot," Christian said. "It's down in the gulley, out of sight from the road. There's no one around. That's where I go to cry."

Dr. Gray shot Andrew a piercing glance, but they both nodded their ascension to the boy's idea.

"Christian!" shouted his mother from the house. "Christian! Come inside, please. Your father is asking for you! Now!"

A desolate expression filled the boy's face. "I'll be right back," he said. He opened the cabin door and rushed up the path to his family's huge home.

The gulley Christian spoke of lay a quarter of a mile behind the house beyond the garden and a low hill. A little creek trickled at the bottom of a ten-foot ditch.

A careful scan of the visible horizon told Andrew they were alone.

He found several dead twigs of varying thickness and set them to rest in a crack on a boulder not one hundred yards from where the doctor stood.

"I won't do it," the doctor said. "You know that."

Andrew returned and stood close. "How will you defend yourself out here? I worry so about you, dear friend."

"And I you," the doctor responded.

Andrew glanced at their surroundings and then back at the doctor. "If we are to survive out here. If we are to protect ourselves from that man who once loved me and the malicious forces he has unleashed against us to avenge his name, what are we to do?"

"Guns are not the answer," the doctor replied after a moment.

"For people like us, they are a necessity." Andrew handed the doctor the gun. "Watch your thumb. Hold it down here. The trigger cocks like this. Aim through the site like I'm doing. Hold the gun out so. Use both hands. It's going to be loud. Blow that first branch off the boulder."

"That Little Gentleman's Academy was some school."

"Little gentlemen were required to learn dueling," Andrew said.

"I told you I won't do it," the doctor repeated. "I loathe guns." The doctor rested his left hand on Andrew's shoulder, and his other hand lowered the gun. "Wouldn't it be wiser to go to the authorities? You've done nothing illegal. They could protect you."

"Like hell," Andrew said. "You and I both know no one gives a fig about the two of us. I played it the way my father wanted me to. What did it get me? Jail. A woman my father paid to be my wife. An allowance if I behaved myself in public. I let that happen because I wanted a safe life. Fool that I was."

"Or just practical."

"Like you?" Andrew said.

"What's wrong with me?" the doctor asked.

"Don't you get tired of it?"

"You know I do."

"That's why we have to fight," Andrew said.

"No, we don't have to fight." The doctor stiffened. "We just have to get to Utopia."

"I was on the front page of the *New York World*, Troy," Andrew said. "In that horrid list of inverts! I wasn't even at that warehouse for their damned party, and they published my name anyway. The Senator's paranoid, and he thinks I'm going to tell someone about him. It's all lurid."

The doctor looked sick. "You're not, are you?"

Andrew snorted once, almost a chuckle. "It's tempting."

The doctor shook his head. "You invite problems."

"And you hide from them." Andrew took the gun from the doctor. "This whole Utopia town idea is one big hideout from the world. I like it less and less the more I think about it."

"It might save your life," was the doctor's indignant response.

"You have a job waiting for you. I have nothing." Andrew sited a twig along the barrel and fired.

The doctor jumped with the explosion of the charge. His ears rang from the blast.

Andrew observed the remaining piece of charred twig drop from the boulder where he had hit it. He lowered the firearm. "Those brandies in New York with you were the only peace I think I ever had, until I met the damned Senator." A darkness fell across Andrew's features.

"It will take a long time to recover from being betrayed like that."

"Especially if he succeeds in killing me." Andrew held out the revolver for the doctor.

The doctor waved it away.

Andrew's eyes grew red around the rims. He glared at the doctor looking for a hope of persuasion. He found none. His expression hardened and he faced the target again and aimed. As he fired he let out a shout.

"Are those gunshots?" Christian Joseph St. Martin's mother asked as the short claps tore the air from the gulley.

"Target shooting. The boarders are target shooting," Christian answered.

Everyone stood gathered around the Reverend St. Martin's deathbed.

"Could we please open a window?" Christian asked. "It smells...so stuffy in here."

"The inverts and Blacks are shooting guns? On my property?" the Reverend rasped. "Get them away from here, away from our holy chapel."

The Reverend began a sickening choking noise from deep inside his chest.

"He's dying!" shouted one of Christian's older sisters. "Just talking about inverts got him to dying!"

"Get that doctor!" Christian's mother told him.

"No!" The Reverend grabbed her arm. He fought and he kicked his legs underneath the starched white sheets. His face became gray.

"Help us, Jesus!" shouted Christian's older sister.

Several of the church people rushed to the pantry for water and towels.

The struggling from the deathbed grew more animated and loud. Christian's mother held the dying man as he fought to get out of bed.

Christian's eyes opened very wide as through the white lace curtain of the window facing south, he witnessed a huge brown-haired stranger lumbering across the pasture toward the gulley. In his hand dangled a gun. "No!"

At that moment, Christian heard his father make a sound he had never heard before. A long tired gasp. A death rattle.

His mother stared at the Reverend in amazement and despair and gently laid him back in bed.

But Christian burst outside, running across the field toward the gulley.

To avoid the din of worrying in his head, Goiter knew sometimes he had to simply move. Fight or run or shoot or strangle. Just move! He had heard the gunshots. He gripped his own gun. All he needed was the element of surprise.

Some would call it a mad dash, but Goiter called it running with a purpose. His ankles almost twisted on the dirt clods in the field, but he was used to dirt clods having grown up on the farmland of Prussia, and he moved quickly behind the house toward the gulley. He hoped the fop was the one shooting the gun and that he was alone or with the strange little doctor because later he could say that he had tried to stop a duel, or hell, he could say just about anything because no one would see him down in the creek. No one would see him kill the fop, and probably the doctor, too.

Goiter felt glee. No one knew he was there. The fop would be taken by surprise. It was perfect. He could go home after that.

He saw no one coming from the house. He only heard the gun-shots. Regular. *Maybe target shooting,* he thought. He reached the lip of the gulley and threw himself down flat on the dirt behind a short rise and the cornstalks. Very carefully he peeked above the outcrop at the creek bed below.

There stood the fop, in that ridiculous shiny blue coat. His back faced Goiter. The other man's back also faced Goiter as the second man spoke with the fop.

The light of ten suns shone on Goiter at that moment. Mission accomplished. He slowly raised his Colt.

The explosion happened as he lowered his eye to the gun site. He felt the bullet enter his left shoulder with a thuck. Down below, as he dropped his gun, he saw the fop staring dead up at him, his own gun still aimed at Goiter with a thin wisp of smoke rising from the barrel. The fop's eyes were trained square on Goiter and the eyes were cold.

His shoulder felt wet and began to ache sharply.

"Mr. Bolding!" Christian Joseph St. Martin shouted from a few yards behind.

"Stay back!" Andrew warned.

"I surrender!" Goiter struggled to hold up both hands for the fop to see.

"I've got his gun!" Christian cried out. He had stooped down to the right of Goiter and retrieved the fallen firearm. "Don't move!" He turned the gun on the big man.

By the time the doctor had climbed to the gulley's lip and examined Goiter's bleeding wound, Goiter found himself staring at black French boots.

"Remember me, Goiter?" Andrew said, as puffy white clouds floated above his head. "Clay Van Torte. But now they call me Andrew Bolding."

The mother shrieked for the boy from her back porch.

"Give me the gun," Andrew told Christian. "Now."

Rather than wait for him to hand it to him, Andrew reached down and took it away.

There were four or five persons gawking from the back porch of the house.

"It's gauche for a boy to carry around a gun," Andrew told Christian. He handed the Colt to the doctor who received it with much opprobrium and placed his Remington in his outside coat pocket.

"Gauche?"

"Will he live?"

After removing Goiter's jacket, Dr. Gray ripped a sleeve from Goiter's tattered wool shirt and wound it into a tourniquet. "Yes. He's lucky." He looked up at Andrew. "That was some shot. He almost killed you."

"Stop smiling, boy," Andrew told Christian. "Come with me."

They hustled back to the house. Christian's mother descended the steps to the dusty yard and took her boy in her arms. After a moment she gripped his shoulders and faced him eye to eye on his own level. She brushed bits of dirt from his white shirt collar. "Your father is dead."

They watched Christian, but he shed no tears. He completed a dry swallow and wriggled free from his mother's hold.

"What about that man?" the sister asked. "Is he dead? God, is everybody dying all around us?"

"Constance, get a hold of yourself."

"I'll get the police," the handsome younger deacon offered.

"No need to get the police," Andrew said.

But the young deacon ignored him and hurried toward the front hallway and the door.

Andrew cocked his Remington, and the sister screamed.

The young deacon turned around in astonishment.

Andrew repeated, "There is no need to get the police."

Outside, Dr. Gray helped Goiter to his feet. They made their way back to the St. Martin house. A flock of crows rose behind them with much ruckus and headed west, out of sight.

"Let's everyone sit down," Andrew told the family and the church people. They all took seats around the foot of the dead man's couch. The mother and her two daughters on a long copper-colored davenport, and the two deacons on plain wooden chairs by the fireplace. Christian Joseph sat next to Andrew on a comfortable upholstered orange divan that featured small crucifixes carved into the wooden arms. Dr. Gray and Goiter took chairs near the deacons.

"My husband has just died," Mrs. St. Martin said with a high, strained voice. "How dare you come into my home with a gun and this vagrant and track blood on my carpets right before the body of my –" Her voice cracked, and she covered her mouth with her hand.

"I am deeply sorry for the rude invasion of your home," Andrew said. "You see, we must be allowed to leave without interference from the police." Andrew's attention remained on Goiter. He leaned heavily on a large serving table, his head in his hands. Blood had soaked through his tourniquet.

"I'll need some assistance dressing this man's wound after I remove the bullet," said Dr. Gray.

"Go out to the cabin with him," Mrs. St. Martin said. "My daughter will help you."

"No, mama! Please! No! I will faint. I will be sick," cried the elder sister.

"How will you learn to be a nurse?" The mother's eyes remained focused solely on the motionless form of her husband.

"I will learn to be a nurse in school, not in a cabin with a man who smells and a scrawny Black invert."

"I am not an invert!" protested Dr. Gray. He got to his feet and took Goiter by the good arm. Goiter yelped in pain and began a slow moan. "Move or we shoot you in the head," Dr. Gray warned, and they began to walk toward the back door and the cabin beyond. "I'll need hot water and alcohol."

As the older daughter scurried off to the kitchen, Andrew said, "Stay where I can see you, young lady."

"My husband could identify inverts by sight," the mother said. "He had written a pamphlet."

"He was either very frightened or very successful at meeting men." Andrew glanced at the dead Reverend's bed and his face. "He wasn't half-bad looking."

Mrs. St. Martin's mouth did not close for several moments. Her younger daughter began to cry softly.

"Who are you?" the older of the two deacons demanded.

"A newspaper item. A user, if you will. A bug that needs extermination."

"Why did you shoot that other man?" the young handsome deacon asked.

"The other man was following him, Mr. Sturges," Christian said. "The other man is a –"

"Business associate," Andrew interrupted.

At this, the mother burst out in a loud wail, rose from her chair, and lay her head on her husband's chest. Her youngest daughter, alarmed at the severity of the emotion, ran to her mother and tugged at her skirt.

"We are passing through," Andrew told the men. "Let us go without word to the police. I might respect your faith."

The older deacon shook his head with disapproval.

Andrew did not anticipate the feelings he felt as the stern bland man ignored his entreaty. The feelings were certainly out of proportion to the circumstances. Perhaps they had built up over the years. It was the same volcanic rage that made him the "Beater of the Bowery."

He stood up and, somewhat giddy with new excitement, pointed the gun at the older deacon. "You're going to give me all the money you have, and so will your handsome associate, and then I will tie you up and gag your mouths, and not before I kiss those full lips of yours, young sir," he said this last bit to the hot potato.

The mother stopped wailing and smoothing out her skirt, unbent herself from over the corpse. "What about us?" She hugged her little girl. "Are we to be tied up, too?"

"Yes. But not before we remove the rings from the hand of your dead husband."

3. An Unexpected Alliance

Goiter lay on his back on the big feather bed in the cabin. "Why are you helping me?" he asked Dr. Gray.

"I'm a doctor."

"I would have killed you," Goiter told him.

"Doesn't scare me. Living is what scares me."

"I can't stand the thought of dying and pain. Especially pain! I can't feel my arm. Will it fall off?" Goiter asked.

"If the arm falls off, I'll stitch it back on."

Goiter lost the desire to converse when he saw the metal forceps the doctor removed from his bag.

"Here is the hot water and rags," the daughter said, as she entered the cabin.

"Thank you, sweet thing," Dr. Gray said. "I'll need you to stay in here with me. Hold this man down."

"Hold me down?" The worry machine that was Goiter's mind began spinning.

The girl rolled up the sleeves of her white blouse. "I've held down a sheep during sheering season before."

"Sorry 'bout this," Dr. Gray told Goiter. "I used up the last of my morphine with the Reverend."

The daughter visibly shuddered. Her eyes became moist.

Pain? thought Goiter. *Not little pain but big pain?* Despite the lava fire in his shoulder and the sweat pouring from his towering forehead, Goiter wanted to leap up from the bed and run through the cow fields all the way back to the train station. *Pain? Why was it necessary to experience more pain?* When he was a child in Prussia he had been run over by a cheese wagon. His right leg had been broken below the knee. The doctor who was also a blacksmith gave Goiter a rag to bite on while the leg was being set. Goiter remembered seeing the planet Jupiter up close that day.

"My poor father!" cried the daughter. "I must go to him."

"He's passed on, my darling." Dr. Gray grabbed the daughter's hands and placed them on Goiter's forearms. "This won't take long." The doctor reached for some rubbing alcohol and a piece of cotton.

Pain? As Goiter's arms were held down at his sides by the pretty girl, he thought of the day in 1843 when he fell down a well near Corntow. He had broken two teeth and his pants had torn off on the way down. He lay in the murky slop at the bottom and called out for help. After half an hour, up above, he heard his mother exclaim to a neighbor. "The well? Goiter's fifteen. He's too old to fall down a well. What kind of idiot would fall down a well at the age of fifteen?"

"I'm here, mother!" Goiter called. It took another ten hours and all of the villagers and a German Shepherd who also fell down the well, before Goiter was pulled free.

The touch of the alcohol on Goiter's bullet wound caused him to moan like a cat.

Dr. Gray had removed perhaps twenty bullets in the war and another five or so at New York Hospital. It was like bobbing for apples with a fork.

"I can't hold him!" cried the daughter. "Stop struggling!" she warned Goiter.

Goiter kicked his legs and clutched at the daughter's white sleeves.

"Stop yelling!" Dr. Gray exclaimed. "I've got the bullet. There!"

Goiter passed out.

"I have to go to my father!" cried the daughter, and she fled out the door, not bothering to clean the spattered blood from the front of her blouse.

Dr. Gray stared at the empty doorway for a moment after. The room was still. His free hand ran over the front of his coat and unbuttoned one button and then another. He could easily remove the bindings and the phony beard and walk out the door like the daughter had just done. The bindings and the beard had given him power for so many years he had lost count. He was tempted more than ever.

He let the bullet fall from the forceps onto a small metal tray with a ping.

The mother wept in the arms of the older deacon.

"How can you do this?" the man asked Andrew with a deep guttural voice.

"I am behaving as the Reverend expected an invert would behave. And as his wife expects, also, I might add."

Andrew stripped the corpse of its wedding ring and the onyx set in silver on the dead reverend's right ring finger. He made an ugly corpse.

"Why don't you take the gold fillings out of his mouth, too?" the hot potato younger deacon said.

"Rings and fillings are not the same things, young man," Andrew said.

"You leave this woman nothing. The family's debts are too great."

"Your church will care for this family. It's a church of love, is it not? That is, love for non-inverts?"

"My husband gambled away our money!" the mother wailed. "He played cards in the basement. With you, Deacon! Both of you!" She indicated the hot potato as well. "And men from the docks. Hard men with cigars! He gambled away our slaves."

Christian Joseph rolled his eyes and glanced at Andrew.

"How am I to get on without a slave?" the mother blubbered. "We'll have to dust our own tables and rinse our own petticoats. We'll have to dig my husband's grave ourselves. We'll have to slaughter our own pigs. I've never slaughtered a pig!"

"Neither have I." Andrew tried on the onyx ring and admired it in the dull light. "Though a pig tried to slaughter me out by the gulley just now."

"No one wants to rent our cabin," the mother went on. "It's a perfectly good room."

"Under the circumstances," Andrew said, inspecting the bric-a-brac whilst keeping his gun trained on the populated side of the dining chamber, "I must forego your lovely room and board. The doctor and I are leaving town. We're taking the wounded behemoth who tried to kill me along with us."

"Where are you going?" Christian Joseph asked.

"Into your storybooks, my dear boy. Now help me find some rope so I can tie up your family."

Andrew had never tied up a family before. It was such a bore. The trick was winding the rope around each of them to cocoon them.

Christian Joseph showed him a hogtie knot he had read about in his books. They used the family's good cloth holiday napkins for gags. When the older daughter ran up the stairs and into the house, she gasped and quivered, first when she beheld her mother bound and gagged, seated on the floor in the center of the parlor, and second when she observed Andrew's gun trained directly on her.

After some time, Dr. Gray marched Goiter at gunpoint up the steps and through the backdoor of the house.

"I could have used your help," Andrew told Goiter as he finished tying the hands of the daughter. The family and the two deacons sat gagged and cocooned in the center of the huge parlor near the buffet table.

"They need blindfolds," Goiter advised with a hoarse voice.

The lumbering leviathan was correct. Blindfolds! Of course.

Andrew meandered up to where the hot potato sat, his sky-blue eyes glaring. "I hate to cover up such a beautiful pair of eyes," Andrew told him. "Just as much as I hated to stuff a napkin between those full young lips. Ah, it is a little appreciated fact that male beauty is sometimes all the more striking in the heat of anger, albeit it misguided." Andrew ran the back of his right hand along the youth's smooth cheek and savored the sensation. "I could take you," Andrew whispered to him. But, instead, he tied a yellow cooking apron around the young man's eyes, and when he was satisfied it was secure, he patted him gently on top of the head.

"What about me?" Christian Joseph asked. He stood with his back to the window.

"Still think I'm some kind of a hero?" Andrew said.

Christian didn't move.

"Andrew!" Dr. Gray exclaimed from the doorway with a horrified look in his eyes.

"It all has to be," Andrew concluded at last.

"What about him?" Dr. Gray indicated Goiter with his gun. "Are you serious?"

Andrew's gaze wandered to the dead man lying in his bed, his face to the ceiling. "We do have some problems, don't we?" He turned away from the cocooned hostages and walked slowly toward Goiter.

Everyone stepped back into the outer room, the boy included, and Andrew shut the door so they had privacy.

"The Senator sent you after me, is that right?"

Goiter kept his mouth closed, but he puffed his cheeks out a bit.

"Answer me."

"I was supposed to kill you."

"My wife supplied you with my most private information?"

Goiter appeared astonished.

"Don't think I didn't know that Tulip was running out to buy her ratty vegetables at all hours of the night just to give you information about my fights in the Bowery, or the parties I went to. I knew. I followed her long ago. And I saw you, Goiter, selling broccoli! There's a hot one! You don't remember me? The accountant from the gang? You don't remember me?"

Goiter squinted. "You were a spy, Martin said. You quit the gang. A political senator wants you dead, but that's all Martin told me."

Andrew grinned a bit and nodded. "That's right. Martin doesn't care a mouse's foot for you. He figures you'll kill me for the Senator, and then you'll be hung in whatever city you happen to be in. Case closed. And you fell for it."

Goiter blinked cow eyes. "Why did you let me live?"

"I don't know."

"Anyone else would have killed me," Goiter said. "You hit me right in my gun shoulder. That was no accident. You could have killed me, and then your doctor stitched me up. You saved my life."

"Don't be so sure."

"Martin wouldn't have saved my life," Goiter said. "No one in the gang would have. I must repay you."

"Repay me? What money do you have?"

"I'll steal some."

"I can steal my own money, thank you," Andrew said.

"Two can work better than one."

"Not if one of the two is an idiot."

"So, you think I'm an idiot." Goiter appeared crestfallen.

Andrew opened the door to the outer room.

"Tie the boy up," he told Goiter. "And gag him."

"No!" Christian shouted.

"Do it," Andrew told Goiter. "And then you can work for me."

"Work for you?" Dr. Gray said, astonished.

"You think people are going to become more tolerant of a mad fop and his Black doctor the farther west we go? And what shall we find in Utopia?"

Dr. Gray felt his teeth clench.

"Where is the rope?" Goiter asked.

Christian Joseph made a dash for the back door, but Goiter reached out and grabbed his collar. He gave the boy a hard yank back.

"Don't tie me up!"

"The rope is in the parlor with the family, on the floor," Andrew said.

Goiter dragged a shouting Christian Joseph away.

"Don't hurt that boy!" Andrew called after them.

"Sit down," Goiter commanded Christian Joseph when they were inside the parlor near the five cocoons that contained the boy's family and two deacons.

Goiter stopped still when he saw the couch and the dead man.

"My father died today," Christian Joseph said with vitriol.

Goiter held the boy fast, but his countenance softened. "My father died as well. It's a hard thing."

"Don't tie me up," Christian Joseph pleaded.

Goiter looked down at the boy. He pushed the boy's shoulders so the boy sat cross-legged on the floor next to the younger deacon cocoon. Goiter kneeled down close to the boy and stretched the rope tightly between his hands. "I was tied up once," Goiter said. "It's not so bad. They tied me up in Prussia after I stabbed my teacher. I hated school."

Christian Joseph's eyes widened. "You've killed people?"

"Yes. But not my teacher. He didn't die. He wasn't able to teach again, but he didn't die. They took me to a children's prison and tied me up. There were all sorts of horrid little boys and girls that had done all sorts of terrible things."

"Like you?"

Goiter felt his forehead tense. "Killing isn't a bad thing."

Several of the cocoons began to struggle and mumble into their gags.

Christian Joseph focused his attention on his two hands, folded in his lap. "My father said I needed to get out in the fresh air more. I didn't like going outside with the other kids at the church school. They called me 'fatty' and 'sissy' and 'ugly Christian.'"

"You're not any of those things," Goiter said.

"Well, I don't play sports well. And I have this round nose that I hate. I don't know. I like books better than people. I wanted to be a writer someday, but my parents said fiction writing is the work of Satan."

Goiter had heard the same thing, but he chose not to say anything.

"The only writing is God's writing. That's what father told me. Can I go with you?"

"Your place is with your family."

Christian Joseph's face lost its color. The light went out of his eyes. The boy became dead silent as if he had been told he would hang at dawn.

"Let me tie you up." Goiter placed a steadying hand on Christian Joseph's shoulder.

The thirteen-year-old's composure melted away. His eyes became wet. "Stay with my family? My family believes everything we do is planned by God in some huge ledger book, and that God lives in a kingdom of gold floating high in the sky surrounded by Angels and Elves and Pixies and flying chariots!"

"What about your mother?" Goiter asked. "She'll need you now your father's gone."

"My mother has someone already!" the boy snarled. "He's a deacon at our church. He's going to take over for my father, and he's going to raise me as his son and make me into some kind of bare-walls do-good-er. I'll sing in the choir. Do you know how much I hate singing in choirs? They make you wear a tissue around your neck and sing real high notes like you're a girl, and they make you practice for hours and hours."

"She's your mother," Goiter said. He remembered his own mother, whom he had left behind in Prussia so many years before.

Christian Joseph's unraveling continued. "She's my step-mother. My real mother's dead. My stepmother doesn't care about me. She wants me locked up in a choir practice chamber and scrubbed with lye. She calls me 'the annoying little creature.'"

And then Goiter watched as the boy drew back in horror realizing that his mother and family were sitting next to him mute and prisoners. He glanced around the house's parlor as if seeing it for the first time. In the doorway to the pantry stood Dr. Gray and the fop.

Goiter stretched the rope and took the boy's hands in his.

Christian Joseph shouted to the fop, "Take me with you! I can carry your luggage. I can be your personal secretary! I want adventure! I want to sail on a raft! I want–"

"Listen, boy..." Dr. Gray hurried toward Christian Joseph and grabbed him by the shoulders and held him still. "It's all fine to want to live your own life. You told us you're only thirteen. We can't take care of you. You can't go with us."

"I know you're a woman," Christian Joseph shouted.

An unearthly silence followed. Andrew joined the little gathering and squatted next to Goiter.

Dr. Gray and the boy had locked eyes.

"I'll tell everyone," Christian Joseph continued. "I'll tell everyone in this city. I'll tell the police. Take me with you."

Goiter glanced at the doctor and watched her slowly lower her hands, releasing the boy. The doctor kept her eyes focused directly on the boy's. "Is that the kind of boy you are?" the doctor asked, finally, in a morose tone. "A boy that would abandon his family and betray two people that never did a thing to him?"

Christian Joseph fidgeted.

The doctor became razor-direct. "Because if that's the kind of person you are, then you deserve everything you get. I don't care what you tell people. You'll end up back where you started, with a woman that doesn't want you and a stone church for a playground. They'll burn your gunslinger books because I'll tell them you've got them. Is that what you want? A life worse than it was before? You think it's bad now? Well, life can always get much, much worse. You don't know how bad it can get. Go ahead. Tell everyone what you think."

Tears began to drip from Christian Joseph's eyes. One trickled to the collar of his white shirt.

"Bring him along," the fop said to the horror of the doctor, and Goiter released the boy's hands.

4. THE ROUGH TONIC

They rode the steamboat to Hannibal and then another train south to St. Joseph. Andrew slept while the unhappy doctor watched Goiter, and Goiter felt uncomfortable. Christian Joseph clutched the small bag filled with books they had let him pack. His eyes grew wide with every mile and every new sight.

Arriving in St. Joseph, disembarking from the train, Andrew drank heavily from his flask under the doctor's disapproving gaze. Fragments of corrosive thoughts cut his mind. What did anything matter now that Senator Hawkins was gone? The "I'm fed up with trying" feeling returned that had driven him to brawl in the alleys of the Bowery. The relationship with the Senator had been the only thing to keep him from those dark feelings. The lying and sneaking around seemed worth it if precious hours with the Senator were the reward. The miserable life in New York had become bearable if only for a short time.

And the Senator had promised more.

Instead of slogging through the mud of a frontier town, Andrew would have been working on an upstate New York farm, ostensibly as the Senator's personal secretary, but of course, as much, much more. Both would have retained their positions, and their marriages would have remained intact in the city with women who both had accepted long ago the hollow trade off of social climbing. He would have traveled abroad with "The Hawk." They had both loved the land, and the farm would have provided them with...

Andrew took another deep draw from his flask. It was useless to ruminate further on what would have been if his name hadn't been published in the paper, or on the ugly fight he had had with the Senator when he had been released from jail.

How quickly love could be traded for status.

He forced himself to notice his surroundings.

All around them people hurried back and forth between the ragtag town and the flowing Missouri River. Two steamboats loaded and unloaded freight, animals, and people. The air smelled of fresh cut timber and smoke from bonfires burning along the riverbank. Mud and manure stank in the gutters of the hastily drawn-together streets.

"Who are these people you've brought with us?" the doctor asked him when they had a moment alone. "We've kidnapped a boy and befriended a murderer. The boy's family is sure to send law enforcement after us. How does it look for a Black man to have robbed a white family with someone who bound and gagged them? They will throw me at bounty hunters who will lie and say I belong elsewhere. What danger have you placed me in?"

He could give the doctor no answer. The very tumult of his own mind made him angrier with himself, made him detest himself more.

He wanted to lash out at his friend, but a bittersweet feeling flooded his chest when he remembered their long ago adventures together in New York City. The doctor had sought him out for forays into the stranger parts of Manhattan, but why, Andrew never really knew. They watched out for each other in questionable dance halls and secret invert ale rooms and more than a few times the doctor made sure Andrew got home in one piece. He was the only one who knew her secret, maybe that was it. And she knew his.

But those days were long gone. There were important plans to be made, and he was sick of plans.

Without further words, he left the doctor and the boy with the task to find a room, and he took Goiter with him into the claptrap streets.

Goiter followed Andrew like a hungry dog, through the dark morning lanes of St. Joseph, through the mud and horse muck to the riverfront east of the ferry landing, where the thugs and thieves spent their off hours.

Andrew stomped past shops and clumps of poor families anxious to find supplies and cross the river. He was going to find a loudmouth who wanted to fight him. He imagined he was going to earn money and help his little entourage outfit itself for the journey to Utopia. He almost believed it.

What he really wanted was to feel the adrenaline. To feel the smack in the face and the blood burning. To lose himself and shut off his mind. Life could be made bearable with overwhelming physical sensations. And he knew just where to get them.

"Wait up!" called Goiter from behind him. Goiter had noticed during the long ferry and train trip that Andrew spent more time talking to Christian Joseph. Why? What was wrong with Goiter? He had all sorts of things to say to someone if they'd only let him.

Goiter wondered if he should kill the boy with the notebook. The idea was exciting. However, killing the boy would anger Andrew, and it would anger the doctor. Goiter fought the craving and busied himself scratching his dirty brown hair. *Maybe*, Goiter thought, *I should make friendly conversation with Andrew.*

On a rutted dirt road along the water he asked, "Did you know your doctor friend was a woman?"

"Of course I did, you fool."

"I'm not a fool!" This was why Goiter had so few friends. He had no idea what friends talked about. "Have you been with many women?"

"I prefer men."

Goiter was flabbergasted. He had heard of such things in prison, but had known no one who chose to live that way out in the world at large.

"If you are to work for me, Goiter," Andrew continued. "Then you must understand that about me and we will get along splendidly."

Goiter stopped walking.

"What is it?" Andrew asked.

"Do you prefer me?" Goiter grew white as a sheet.

"No, Goiter. Not an atom of you! I would sooner eat spoiled fish or hit my own head with a hammer. The very idea makes my skin crawl."

Goiter appeared relieved, but only momentarily. "The gang will send another assassin out for the both of us, unless we can send back proof that I killed you."

"You worry too much."

They stopped abruptly at a row of uneven wood structures that alone blocked them from the riverbank. Some of the buildings stood on stilts over the water; others sat squat on the earth.

There were all manner of men and boys in ragged clothes and hats milling about the different buildings. Many of them reacted to the sight of Andrew with alert interest.

Goiter gasped. "We're outnumbered."

"You'd do best not to open your stupid mouth," Andrew said. "Let me do the talking and when I tell you to return to town without me, you'll do as I say."

"I know my way around," Goiter said with indignation. "You should have given my gun back to me."

Andrew shot Goiter a glare made more intense by the black pencil around his eyes. Goiter submitted.

They walked right up to the thickest cluster of men. As always, there was an almost polite silence as the men looked Andrew over. He knew this from New York. There would be some who welcomed him as a glittery bauble or an exotic Toucan – and try to fleece him of his money or use him in some other way. There would be others who would ignore him with contempt. And there would be those that approached him with fear or disgust, because they were like Andrew inside.

"Did ya fall out of a carriage, Miss?" a pug-nosed punk said. "That coat's seen its share, ain't it?"

There was a smattering of laughs.

"No more than your face," Andrew answered.

Pug-Nose liked that answer. "Who's this rabbit eyes?"

"His name is Goiter."

"He's bleedin' through his shirt."

"It's nothing," Goiter said.

The Pug-Nose handed Andrew a smoky blue bottle. Andrew took a healthy swig and handed it back. The men around him relaxed and most of them drifted away, but Pug-Nose stayed. "I can get you anything you want. This is my gang, The River Royals."

"Catchy name."

"You ever been in a gang?" Pug-Nose gave Goiter a once-over. "This big one has, I'll bet."

Goiter frowned.

"What is it you want?" Pug-Nose asked Andrew again. "Here at River Royale."

Andrew glanced around the chimneystacks and broken wagons and tools. Goiter watched him with what looked like dread. Andrew motioned for the man to hand him back his bottle. As Andrew took it, the man winked once at him.

"We need money and horses," Andrew said.

"Nothing's free," Pug-Nose answered.

Andrew nodded slightly in agreement.

Pug-Nose put his arm around Andrew's shoulder and sneered again at Goiter. "He'd need a big one, a Clydesdale."

Goiter's mind was all atwitter with anxieties and half-formed worries. As a boy in Prussia, he had not ridden a horse, but he'd ridden oxen. Oxen were easy to ride. They were wide in the middle, and they moved slowly so falling off was more like tilting over. But a horse was different. A horse could run and gallop, and it was tall, and you had to lean forward, and there were so many details to the entire endeavor that Goiter would become overwhelmed.

"How did you think we were going to get around out west?" Andrew asked, when the pug-nosed bully had gone off to confer with several of his associates in a mud alley. "Men ride horses out there. What if we are attacked by Indians or bandits? We'll have to move quickly. Did you think we would just run through the prairie dirt clods on our own two feet?"

Goiter hadn't said a word, yet it seemed that Andrew was having an argument all on his own.

The pug-nosed thug invited them into an abandoned ferry building. Inside, pockets of light from holes in the ceiling adding spots of color to the several gang members inside. A red shirt there, a yellow hat there. The small building dated back to the days before the gold rush. The interior was cluttered with battered half-open steamer trunks, crates, boxes, and rumpled clothing on the dusty wood floor.

"Where out west are you headed?" Pug-Nose asked.

"Utopia," Andrew answered.

"Heard of that," Pug said. "Whole town of deviants. My kind of place."

"Lots of 'em communes out yonder," a voice muttered from dusty boxes against the wall.

"Yup," Pug said. "New worlds. They say there's a city of Little People out there. We met a few of them last month takin' the ferry 'cross the river. And Mormons with five hundred wives. Yeah, Utopia's just one of 'em places."

"Have you met other people going to Utopia?" Andrew asked.

The pug-nosed boy stopped inside the gray light of a dusty sunbeam. "Probably. Not one done up like you, though."

Goiter began to perspire. He was aware of maybe ten men in a large circle surrounding him and Andrew. He glanced at Andrew, but the fop didn't appear surprised. Perhaps the fop had expected or even wanted this confrontation. *But why?* wondered Goiter.

Goiter had never fought ten men at once. The arithmetic did not bode well. Even though Goiter murdered people for money and to fill a deep-seated craving, he only murdered one person at a time and only when he had the advantage.

The men surrounding them began to close in the circle.

Goiter moved to fight.

Andrew reached out a hand and held Goiter's arm. "Who will fight me? Alone in this circle?" Andrew stripped off his blue velvet jacket, gun, white French dress shirt, and undershirt until he was bare-chested before the river gang.

Goiter was shocked at the fop's athletic physique. He prepared himself to throw the clothing to the ground and begin fighting when the pug-nosed kid raised one hand.

No one moved any farther.

"I'll fight you," and to his gang he shouted, "Give us room!"

The men and boys backed off to the shadows of the old ferry building. Andrew handed Goiter his gun. Goiter moved back. Three gray shafts of light from the ceiling illuminated the uneven floorboards that were to be the ring.

Pug-Nose stripped off his soldier's jacket and wool shirt. He was hairy. His grin revealed a missing front tooth.

Goiter thought of the cockfights and the dog fights back in New York. This was no different. But Andrew would earn no money from this fight, so what purpose did it serve?

One of the locals paraded a silver dinner triangle through the center of the ring area and clanged a small copper pipe about the insides before rushing back into the shadows.

Andrew sprang upon Pug-Nose. Goiter heard a collective gasp from the observers. Goiter, himself, was astonished at the speed with which Andrew had attacked.

The two young men rolled on the rotted floorboards. The others cheered and shouted, "Kill 'em, Edgar! Kill the dandy!"

Everyone moved closer in to get a good look around the lip of the circle.

With a deep grunt, Edgar kicked Andrew in the chest and knocked him backwards off of him. Edgar sprang onto Andrew almost as quickly as Andrew had done. Several brutal punches were thrown. Goiter watched Andrew take one in the face directly on the nose. Blood spurted out in a gush and onto Edgar as they wrestled.

Both of the young men's backs became scratched and dirty from the ancient ferry building floor.

Andrew slammed a fist into Edgar's teeth, then rolled them both over and, straddling Edgar, began to pummel the sides of Edgar's head. The sounds made with each punch sickened Goiter.

"Pull 'em off! Pull 'em away!" the River Royals shouted and three of the largest of them moved in toward Andrew and grabbed him under the arms and around the waist. They struggled to lift him, and as Andrew kicked his legs, one of them punched Andrew in the stomach.

Goiter saw how this would go. He could either leave his newfound friend to be beaten to death, or try to save him.

He fired Andrew's gun at the ceiling. During the moment of startled silence that followed he demanded, "Let my friend go."

"Let him go," Edgar repeated, from his position lying on the floor.

The three men let go of Andrew, who immediately slumped to the floor, panting and holding his stomach. His face was swollen and covered with spit and snot and blood.

Goiter noticed the curiosity in many of the faces of the River Royals as they stared at Andrew, the man who did not give up and who in fact, had almost beaten their own leader at a bare knuckles brawl.

"Get them whiskey!" commanded Edgar. He coughed and sat up, covered in sweat and blood. "Whiskey all around!"

Goiter didn't drink. He didn't like what it did to him and though he was always admonished, he refused a drink every time it was offered.

They were on the riverfront until the next morning, drinking, smoking, and when Edgar said he would, "round up some women," Goiter watched with amazement as Andrew told them he preferred a handsome young man, and within fifteen minutes one of the River Royals was at his side.

It was morning and they were seated on the pilings of one of the piers, when Edgar leaned in close to them both and said, "I know how you can get some money and horses."

5. A Change Of Fortune

"Am I dying?" Christian Joseph asked the doctor from his bed in the dingy room.

Again, the unwanted sensation of being a "parent" to a child bristled within the doctor. "Stay quiet," the doctor said. "You must have caught something on the steamboat."

The morning light shone through the cracks between the wallboards. Andrew and the hired lug had not returned.

The doctor realized that what had made Andrew an exciting friend in New York became foolhardy and dangerous on the frontier. Terrible how repression could gnaw at a man over the long years, twisting him into a starved animal that only eats itself sick when at last presented with a meal.

She had thought he could rise above all of that.

Instead of just one child to mother, the truth was she had two. She wanted no part of it.

"What is Utopia like?" the boy asked.

The doctor sat next to him on the bed and wiped his forehead with a cloth. "They say it is free, truly free."

"You could be a woman there?"

The doctor squinted at the boy. "What makes you think I want to be a woman?"

"Aren't you wearing a disguise? People that wear a disguise don't want to be found out about something. What is it you don't want people to find out?"

The doctor pulled back at the remark. The boy's sudden insight was disarming. Her interest in other women wasn't the half of what she didn't want regular people to find out. *It's not just the clothing,* she thought. *I feel like a man. I'm not just in disguise.*

"What's the matter?" Christian Joseph asked.

"What? Nothing." Still, the doctor's thoughts wandered: *My idea of a man and not some of the halfwits I've suffered.*

"Until we get there I'm a man, and you don't say anything about that subject, do you hear?" she said, at last.

Christian Joseph felt too tired to argue.

"You want adventure, don't you?" the doctor said. "Well, I'm your ticket, so you better make me like you."

"I do," and the boy began to doze.

While the boy tossed and turned and coughed, the doctor drew back the rags that functioned as "drapes" and watched the people pass by on the street outside.

Men leading horses with Calistoga wagons pulled behind, clattering on the rough stones of the roadway. Women with children rode in the wagons or walked alongside, in the long procession to the waterfront and the ferry to the open land of Kansas. In the riff raff of the throng, the doctor searched the faces for one that held a kindred expression.

And, in fact, there were several. They were frequently holding children or following their husbands on the roadway leading horses or holding parcels. The younger women were unattached and oblivious to anything but what common social rules had mapped out for them. Every so often, the doctor spied a young woman in a Davy Crocket jacket or with hair cut short, and she trembled as she knew that her journey west was the right one.

Her bindings chaffed her skin this morning and her beard itched. Her costume suddenly felt ridiculous. As much as Dr. Gray aspired to all the advantages men held in society, she did not find attractive all the disadvantages men held in their characters. She found most of them weak, impulsive, and selfish. It was a fine line to want power, prestige, and opportunity and to reject the dark side effects such goals generated.

When the boy asked for some water, the doctor poured some from the flask on the wobbly wooden table into a wooden cup and gave it to him. She mopped the boy's forehead with a clean cloth. She worried the boy had cholera, but so far, the symptoms suggested nothing more than a cold or virus.

Dr. Gray sat on the edge of her bed and watched him quietly. From her pocket she removed a paper with a list she had written up the night before while waiting for Andrew to return – the food, tools, and supplies they would need for their trip to Wyoming.

Andrew and Goiter returned late in the morning. Andrew stripped off his shirt. He stood before the wash basin to rinse his bruises.

"I should look at those," the doctor said without emotion.

"I'm fine." After toweling off with a dry rag, Andrew headed toward one of the cots.

The doctor made a face of disapproval. "Another fight? You might have told us where you went. The kid is sick."

"We're back now." Andrew stared up at the miserable ceiling.

"This isn't one of our poker games back home," the doctor contin-ued. "...or one of our brandies. It's our lives."

"Stop your mothering. I'm gonna get us some money."

The doctor gritted her teeth. "Aren't you tired of breaking the law?"

Andrew groaned as he sat up to face the doctor. "Aren't you tired of wearing that beard?"

The doctor fought to keep her composure. "Don't talk that way to me."

"I'm sorry," Andrew said. "I'm just so sick of everything."

"Of me?"

"No. I can't explain it." He put his hand on his forehead and then dropped back onto the cot. He closed his eyes.

Dr. Gray shook her head in disgust. She folded her arms and crossed the room past Goiter toward the window. Staring out through smudges at the bones of the raw fledgling town, Dr. Gray muttered, "That's the trouble. I've been foolish for relying on him."

Andrew slept through the afternoon, and after a meal of boiled potatoes and lamb purchased from a street vendor, he took some air with Goiter. They sat outside on a bench in the setting sun with a view of the Missouri River in the distance.

"Ain't the rings you stole from the boy's dead daddy enough to pay our way to Wyoming?"

Andrew tilted his head to look at the rings on his left hand and winced with pain from his sore nose. "I intend keeping them."

"You could have been killed last night," Goiter said, as two magpies jibbered and flew from the brush beside their shack. "I don't under-stand you."

"You get cravings to kill people. I get cravings to dip into the barrel of depravity. Same thing."

"You were with that young roughneck, and you'll never see him again."

"I won't say I didn't enjoy him. What's the difference from men seeing female whores?"

"I don't understand it."

"Well, my dear Goiter, I don't understand your pleasure in murdering people. You treat the idea as if it were nothing more than having a brandy after dinner."

"Something much stronger than a brandy," Goiter said, and he kicked a pebble.

"I'll say! I may lie with men, but I don't take their lives!"

Goiter lowered his head.

"Maybe you and I deserved to be in that gang back in Manhattan," Andrew said. "I thought I was better than all of you but obviously I am not."

To the south of them floated the shouts of ferrymen and an occasional snort of distress from cattle.

"You didn't kill me before," Goiter said. "That makes you better. Any of the others would have killed me."

Because I felt sorry for you, fool, thought Andrew. And he took a deep breath when he realized he felt sorry for a murderer.

"The gang will wonder why they haven't heard from me."

Andrew squinted in the sun at Goiter.

Goiter crossed his arms and hunched forward even though there was no chill to the air. "I've run out of time. We probably shouldn't be sitting like this outside."

"No one can see us here. Look, as long as you're with me we'll be fine."

Goiter glanced shyly at Andrew. "I want to believe that. But my brother told me he'd be fine, and he's gone. Carter killed him. I'll never have a brother again!"

Andrew looked down at the minister's rings. "Carter…"

"I'll never forget that day," Goiter said. "The gang is capable of anything. My brother was the only person who gave a damn about me."

Andrew removed a tattered paper Edgar had given him on the pier. He smoothed it out on his leg and read: "Men needed to remove trespassers from property. Must have grit. Good pay. Apply at Wunderfahrt Ranch. Utopia, Wyoming." He nudged the sullen Goiter with his elbow.

"You trust that hoodlum, Edgar?" Goiter asked.

"We're hoodlums, too! This is a real advertisement, and I don't have a job out in Wyoming like the doctor does."

"And the stagecoach idea? Why should he care about us?"

"Maybe he respects us, and that's in short supply for me these days. I'll take it!" Andrew shook the paper at Goiter. "We're headed this way anyway. We'll blend in until this all blows over. I got grit. How 'bout you?"

Goiter slowly nodded that he also had grit.

"Sure you do!" Andrew exclaimed. "What are we gonna do? Farm? Ha! I sure as hell am not going to go back to accounting. This will keep the excitement in our veins!"

Goiter wasn't sure it was excitement he was looking for, but maybe Andrew was right about the wisdom of blending in until the gang didn't care about them anymore.

Christian Joseph drifted in and out of sleep. He was hot. He was clammy. He threw up. He tried to drink water. The room was stuffy.

And all the while, Dr. Gray was nearby, seated in a rough oak chair, placing cold compresses on the boy's forehead or pacing the floor and muttering something that Christian Joseph couldn't quite make out.

He vaguely remembered his hero, Andrew, return and go out. His back ached from lying in bed since the day before and now into a second night. "Am I dying!" he demanded to know.

The doctor came over to the boy's bedside. "You must be patient. Don't you know that's where that word came from in the first place?"

The boy relaxed slightly back onto his damp pillow.

"Here now," Dr. Gray said, wiping the boy's forehead with a clean rag.

"Where is Andrew?"

"He left with Goiter. They said they were going to earn some money."

That sounded strange to the boy. Andrew wasn't the type to get a job. "When is he coming back?"

"God only knows."

A short breath of confusion blew across the boy's face, and then he said, "I don't want to die before I get to see the Wild West. That wouldn't be fair. To run away from home, take a train a couple of stops, catch the flu and die right at the ferry landing on the Missouri! That wouldn't be fair."

"Nothing is fair," Dr. Gray said. "That's the truth."

The boy slept a little bit. He felt a draft of cold air, and he was aware of the doctor letting someone into the room: a man with a black hat and coat and long beard. At first, Christian Joseph couldn't hear what the doctor and the man said, but he caught some of it.

"They did not say you were a Black doctor."

"Why should they?" the doctor said.

"I was cut. Broken glass on the wagon. Careless."

And later..

"...stitches will need to come out in six weeks. Keep it clean."

"What is the charge?"

"Nothing."

A silence. "Why?" the man asked the doctor.

"Perhaps you can find me a job instead."

6. Separate Ways

The colors of the town sparkled in a morning that glowed. The warmth of the spring sun felt good to Christian Joseph, but all of the sensorial pleasures in the world could not erase the void that Andrew Bolding's absence had created.

Andrew and Goiter again had not returned.

"He doesn't see fit to tell us where he went or even to discuss what we are to do next. There is no place for that behavior in the wilderness," the doctor muttered to herself as she soaked a small towel in cold water to place over the boy's forehead. Perhaps Andrew's misguided bravery was something she had once admired. But now his self-destructive behavior had escalated at the same time she wanted to reduce hers.

"Everything depends on my getting to Utopia," she said softly while wringing out the towel. "I can't let anything or anyone risk that happening for me."

The boy and Dr. Gray stood on the dank walkway in the shadows as the Mormon in the dark hat called John approached them both and told the doctor, "All is made ready. We are to leave now. We have procured a guide." He motioned with his hand to a figure in the distance, leaning his elbows on a railing outside a saloon. The figure wore a triangular Daniel Boone hat, and a brown suede jacket with fringe decorating the sleeves. He smoked a pipe and appeared rather bored.

Christian Joseph brightened. Several of his penny westerns had been about brave mountain men: *Whiskers Parker and the Teepee of Death* and *The Ten Stabbings of Idaho Pete* were two of his favorites.

"What's his name?" the boy asked.

"Francis Piggott."

Christian felt clammy. So much for heroic names. He sauntered after Dr. Gray with his small cloth bag of books, feeling renewed after his illness, but angry with himself for idolizing someone like Andrew Bolding.

The emigrants, as they were to be called, boarded a train of eight wagons near the ferry. There were five families. Women outnumbered the men three to one. Children counted at close to twenty. Christian Joseph took Dr. Gray's hand.

"You've played games and read your books. This is the biggest game of all," Dr. Gray whispered to Christian when John had gone ahead to speak to the women on his wagon. "From now on, I am your guardian, and we have been traveling alone from New York. Just agree with everything I say, and keep quiet as much as possible."

"But what about Andrew? We can't just leave him!"

"He's going to catch up to us. He told me so," the doctor lied.

The boy struggled to pull his hand free.

The doctor whirled around and the hardness in her eyes immobilized him.

She noticed his fear and relaxed her grip on his hand. He snatched it away. She marveled at how angry and sad she felt. She reached up to stroke the little silver chain around her neck, remembering the night in a New York alehouse when Andrew had given it to her. At her insistence he had agreed to give up fighting that night. Self-destructive, she had called it. They had not spoken for several days and at last Andrew had made peace.

But it didn't last.

The morning heated the earth. The reality of leaving civilization became palpable. They would cross the Missouri on the ferry and find themselves on the great prairies battling the elements. The wagons stood waiting near the dew-covered shrubs. The doctor felt a tension run down her arms, guilt and anxiety for leaving Andrew without telling him what she was doing. It was the only way. He'd only try to make amends, and she had learned with him that wasn't enough.

He knew where he could find her. She was going there before she ever invited him, anyway.

Still, the guilty feeling gnawed at her.

"I hear you are the sawbones for the group." Francis Piggott smelled of tobacco.

"Yes," Dr. Gray answered.

"You'll be very busy."

"Why? What have you seen?" Christian Joseph asked eagerly. "How many times have you been out there?"

"Quiet, boy!" Dr. Gray said.

Francis Piggott squatted down to be eye level with Christian. "I've seen scalpings. I've seen bullets pass through flesh. I've seen the fever and rattlesnake bites. And look right here..." Piggott lifted the side of his jacket and pulled open his flannel shirt. Huge scars from a large bite, well healed, presented themselves. "Bit by a grizzly."

Christian adjusted his glasses and gasped in admiration. He glanced up at Dr. Gray and was surprised to see the Doctor appeared unimpressed.

Piggott patted the boy on the head and took long confident strides toward the group of Mormons by the front wagon.

"I wouldn't trust him," Dr. Gray advised.

They passed across the Missouri River by early afternoon and at last, the wagons filled with Mormons led by John and Piggott at his side, rattled off along a wheel-rutted trail headed west.

I'm actually leaving for the frontier! Christian Joseph thought to himself as he dangled his legs over the back of the open wagon, the last of the train, which he shared with a cluster of children and two women. *I'm a writer heading west!* He glanced around at the clanging pots and pans suspended from safe hooks and the linens and barrels of dried meat and flour.

It became immediately apparent that most everyone they passed detested them. Several men in buckskin jackets even spit on the ground with disgust as they passed. Women pulled their children back from the wagons with distressed and worried faces.

Christian Joseph glanced up at Dr. Gray seated next to him in the back of the wagon. The doctor looked as if she was debating something in her mind, and she didn't look pleased.

"Most people don't like Mormons," the doctor explained. "They don't like their religion."

Christian Joseph was baffled. Back home in Ohio, his family had been treated with high regard. They received gifts and compliments. People asked Christian's father for favors. Christian had longed to be like other boys. He hated being part of "a model family," treated like royalty but completely misread. Yet he never wished to be spat upon or cast down among the lowest dregs of society in other men's eyes.

He shrugged. No matter. He would become a better writer this way.

He watched the chimney smoke and bustle of St. Joseph become smaller on the horizon and the river that he had crossed on the ferry disappear from view. The wagon jolted over uneven places in the dirt road. Christian hoped he would see a lone rider galloping up to meet them and that it would be Andrew come to join them.

No one came.

"You're not one of us," a boy with bulky limbs and a thick neck said. His skin was white as clay and his expression was one of bridled rage. He had climbed onto the backboard from somewhere inside the wagon.

"Watch yourself," Francis Piggott warned the boy from horseback. He had held himself back at a slower pace to check in with the party. "Kelly's done some bad things," the mountain man told Christian and the doctor. "Don't mind him. I'll give him a good thrashing if he bothers you." And with that, Piggott swacked the boy on the arm with a long bristled switch.

"Eoww!" cried Kelly.

Christian Joseph wondered what "bad things" the other boy had done, but Kelly became mostly uncommunicative for the rest of the day, scowling and rubbing his arm in the shadows of the wagon's interior.

The wagons stopped three times before sundown. Each time, Christian Joseph, Dr. Gray, and Kelly had to hop down in the mud and help push or lift or pull in order to free the wheels from a pit of muck.

"Afraid to get dirty?" Kelly asked after the third hefting of the wagon.

"I've rolled up my sleeves if that's what you mean," Christian said.

Kelly laughed. He couldn't have been more than eleven or twelve, but his laugh sounded like he had smoked cigars for twenty years.

If Andrew were there, he'd know how to handle a boy like Kelly. Christian Joseph wondered where Andrew was and if Andrew even remembered him.

The sun bore down on them throughout the long hours.

The eight wagons of the Mormon emigrants stopped in what formed a sloppy square in the mud. The shadows grew longer on their tenth day of traveling, and the platte breathed cold browns and blacks. Several wolves howled in the distance.

Christian Joseph sat next to Dr. Gray. They ate their supper of beans, beef, and stringy stale cabbage, with John, his three wives, and seven small children.

"I am very unhappy," Wife #2 said.

"You must prepare yourself for what is ahead," John said. He sat at the head of the supper blanket. "We must unload the mahogany dresser. It is too heavy for the mules to pull."

"Yes, sister," Wife #3 said.

"We have so many children!" Marianne, sometimes known as Wife #1, complained. She pulled the edges of her eggshell-colored bonnet tight over her ears and forehead in something of a sulk. "They crawl all over me, and I cannot sleep."

"No matter how grim things may be," John said. "God tells us we must press on. You are only angry, Marianne, because you fell off the sandbank at the river and tore your petticoat."

"I almost severed a vein in my forearm," Marianne shot back.

"That's not exactly true," Dr. Gray put in.

Marianne glared at Dr. Gray. As Wife #1 she had developed a piercing dominating glare. "You are a strange little man," Marianne said. "Why do you not bathe with the other men?"

Dr. Gray poked a twig at the ground. "I am modest."

In fact, in addition to Marianne, Christian Joseph noticed that several of the older girls had kept Dr. Gray constantly under their scrutiny. There was no privacy whatsoever. Not even a grove of trees.

"If it weren't for our gracious doctor," John interjected, "dear wife, you might have bled to death out here in the yawning expanse. How lucky we are to have a real doctor with us. When we ran over Seth with the wagon, our doctor set the boy's leg."

"Yes," Marianne said. "The doctor has gentle hands. He has almost a mother's touch."

Christian Joseph sat leaning against a dirty wagon wheel. He noticed Dr. Gray straighten.

"I've offered to trim his beard in gratitude for what he has done," Marianne said. "But our doctor won't let me touch him. His beard is the strangest I have ever seen. Around the edges it sweats white thick drops in the midday sun."

"Perhaps it is because our doctor works so hard to help us push the wagon through the mud and quicksands," John said.

"I am so unhappy!" Wife #2 exclaimed. "Why must we jettison our beautiful polished dresser?"

"You imbecile!" shouted Wife #3. "We should jettison you instead! In the day it is hot as fire, and I want to tear off my wool dress and this strangling bonnet, and in the night there are not enough blankets to keep me warm."

"I will come to your bed," John said.

"Yes, that will solve all of our problems!" Wife #2 snapped.

"How dare you speak to John that way!" Marianne said.

"My dear wives. You are tired and discouraged. Remember our mission!"

"I got dysentery before our first lunch, John!" Wife #2 said. "And now you say I must part with my mother's mahogany dresser?"

Christian Joseph finished the last of his supper. He wondered where Andrew was. He indulged himself in delineating further in his mind his plan to run away and find Andrew. He would steal one of the horses in the night...but that was as far as the plan went, for he knew not what direction to ride.

The doctor pointed at a dark funnel shape growing larger in the sky. "That's not a normal rain cloud."

Christian Joseph followed the doctor's pointing finger and his eyes widened. "Is that...a typhoon?"

"No. I think they call them tornadoes."

7. The Robbery

On the steamship south from St. Joseph, Andrew hardly spoke. The doctor had never abandoned him before. In that sense, she was now no better than the Senator. A growing fear developed that he had ruined the best friendship he ever had. They had never quantified their relationship. It just was. Andrew considered whether he had become even more selfish than his father had accused him of being, and in so doing, taken for granted the loyalty of Dr. Gray. *I'm tearing myself apart over this. She made her choice. I've always heard the frontier changes people, or it makes them become even more of what they were before. I don't need someone to be my conscience following me everywhere I go. Or do I just want to live without any conscience at all?*

Andrew's steely silence alarmed Goiter. Goiter wasn't concerned about the doctor leaving. In fact, he was glad. Now he'd have the fop's friendship all to himself. They had stayed out another night, conferring with Edgar around his river bonfire, and later Goiter waited as Andrew debauched himself further with the young ruffians. Fine, if that's what it took to have a friend.

In Kansas City, Andrew announced they would initiate Edgar's stagecoach idea.

They boarded the coach in Kansas City. Goiter had only ridden omnibuses in New York and hay wagons back in Prussia. What he hadn't counted on were the extremely tight quarters of a stagecoach. Goiter packed himself inside the carriage with Andrew and two other passengers and bounced and vibrated until what were left of his teeth had loosened considerably and his brain had banged repeatedly against the inside of his sorry skull.

Dust poured inside from the open windows. Closing them only baked the passengers. They stopped numerous times to help push the carriage out of deep ruts of mud.

There were two redeeming features to the stagecoach scheme; the first was Andrew returned Goiter's .45 to him, apparently signaling trust in the former Prussian; the second was the little black strong box containing the wealth of the passengers and whatever moneys were being transported from St. Joseph to Oklahoma City.

Despite a pounding headache, Goiter reviewed Edgar's idea. They were to befriend the other passengers, lull them into dropping their guard, and then hold them up at gunpoint during a rest stop at some deserted water hole, steal the horses, and light out for Wyoming.

Although Goiter wasn't keen on the future job "removing trespassers" from a ranch.

Another option occurred to Goiter: shoot Andrew and all the rest, take the money, and run away from everyone and everything. He sighed in wonder at the thought. That was the old Goiter. The Goiter who had no friends. Now he had Andrew and vowed to protect him.

His seatmate, Mr. Vine, was shaped like an avocado, and perhaps forty years of age. He reminded Goiter of his mother who had been known as the "the most nonathletic woman in Vlkakspazia." Vine's face was pale but handsome. He had all of his hair and none of it was gray. He told them he was from China and that he was a fight promoter traveling with his star client, a woman boxer named Madame La Fleuvre.

La Fleuvre was a short blocky woman from Quebec. She squeezed herself in facing Vine and Goiter leaving Andrew precious little room necessitating his sitting with his knees together. She adorned herself all in pink, including gloves and a hat. She wore too much powder on her face and her blond hair she kept in thick limp ringlets.

"Madame is stronger than any man," Vine said. "I once saw her, wearing this same pink dress, chop up an entire conifer tree in less than two hours. It was a horrific sight! The axe flew with such force and the way she gnashed her teeth...the primal monstrous way she tore off those branches when they began to fall. The woman is fueled by rage."

"Ah. Go on," La Fleuvre scolded. "You sound like your fight posters."

"To be a woman in a man's profession is very brave." Andrew raised his voice over the rattling of the stagecoach.

"Bravery is not the same as skill," Mr. Vine said somberly. "Bravery is often foolish. I imagine that I am brave facing my ultimate end, but it is all delusion, isn't it?"

Goiter wasn't sure what "delusion" meant, but he had once heard Ol' Horace back at Sing Sing use the word to describe Goiter's ability to become a gang commander in the Fourth Ward of the Bowery. *Why waste any more time on small talk?* thought Goiter.

"I have always been popular with men," Madame La Fleuvre boasted. "Ever since I was a girl. I was very strong even as a toddler."

The stage hit a large rock banging all of their heads, except La Fleuvre's, on the ceiling.

"One of my backers from Oklahoma City is in love with me," La Fleuvre went on. "He's a mountain man who has made his fortune in California. He can lift me over his head." She patted her powdered cheeks and examined her pink gloves. She brushed her gloved hands together and wrapped her arms around her folded legs.

Andrew nodded once to Goiter. Goiter recognized it as their signal. Outside in the vastness approaching low hills no one else was visible for as far as they could see.

"I must relieve myself!" shouted Goiter an octave too high. He thrust open the carriage door and called to the driver. "Please stop. I must relieve myself and I don't want the lady to bear witness."

The carriage came to a stop. Goiter jumped to the ground. When he had landed and was out of view, Andrew removed his revolver. "Now, both of you will get out as well," he glanced at La Fleuvre. "... or I will blast the powder off your lips."

Andrew's hands and face tingled as he lined Vine, La Fleuvre, and the driver up against the side of the carriage with their hands on their heads and their backs to Andrew. He rocked the handle of the revolver slowly in the palm of his hand, enjoying the feel of it, savoring the touch, each movement a hot caress. Without the reproaches of the doctor, he could make closer acquaintance with his gun.

He commanded Goiter to remove Vine's steamer trunk from the outside carriage straps. Goiter fumbled with the buckles. The trunk fell and hit the carriage sideboard with a hard thud before landing upside-down in the dirt.

Next, Andrew ordered Mr. Vine to open his trunk and remove all of his money.

Vine turned slowly to face them. "I won't do it."

"You will," Andrew said. "Or I will kill you."

Goiter watched Andrew. Andrew's heartbeat sped up.

"You'd be doing me a favor," Vine said. "Ending this nightmare of a life."

Andrew bit his lower lip. "You're supposed to love this life," he said. "Look around you at the beauty of these plains, of this woman. Open the trunk."

Vine lowered his hands and extended his arms to indicate Andrew could take free aim at his chest with the gun.

"Shoot off the latch," Andrew instructed Goiter, as he kept his gun trained on the three prisoners.

Goiter aimed the gun with both arms extended. The gunshot cracked.

Having missed, Goiter aimed again, and fired. The second shot echoed through the cold silence.

Andrew sighed. "Concentrate, you idiot. Money is no good with holes shot all through it!"

Before Goiter could fire a third time, Andrew exclaimed, "Oh, here, let me do it!"

Andrew made Goiter switch places and train his gun on the three hostages.

He stomped over to the trunk. Resolutely, Andrew stood still, aimed his Remington with one hand, thrilled at the steadiness of his grip, and fired at the lock.

The lock flew off and the lid cracked open, just as La Fleuvre roared like a banshee and rushed Goiter headlong, hitting him in the gut with a bear hug. The two of them toppled to the ground and rolled. Goiter's gun went off straight up into the air.

The carriage driver and Vine both scuttled around to the trembling horses for cover, but Andrew fired and sent a bullet tearing past the driver's right boot, so close that he stumbled and Vine tripped over him. Andrew was behind them in an instant. "Don't move!"

A flurry of pink fabric and Prussian flannel wrestled and grunted and cried out from dry ground nearby. La Fleuvre locked her arm around Goiter's throat and held his body in front of her like a human shield. The veins on Goiter's neck grew red and bulged. His eyes, focused on Andrew, held profound alarm.

La Fleuvre's hat had yanked sharply over her right ear in the fracas. "I've got his gun," she shouted. She pointed Goiter's revolver up at his head with her non-strangling hand. "Let us go or he dies!"

"I don't want to die!" Goiter shouted.

"Shut up!" To La Fleuvre, Andrew said, "I'll kill the driver and Vine, and you'll kill Goiter. Then it will be just us two."

"Sounds good to me!" The woman cocked her gun.

Goiter cried out something in Prussian.

"Do it!" Vine yelled.

The driver fainted.

"Don't help him!" Andrew commanded Vine.

"I've got you beat." La Fleuvre tossed back several stray ringlets of moist hair with a flick of her head. "Vine wants to die, this big one here doesn't. I win."

"If you shoot the big one," Andrew said, "I will shoot you. I don't care about Vine, and he is unarmed. Drop your gun."

"You're not that fast," La Fleuvre said.

But she let Goiter go. Goiter composed himself quickly and hustled across the sloping hillside to stand behind Andrew, away from the nasty woman.

Andrew forced La Fleuvre to tie her pink scarf around Vine's mouth and handkerchief around the driver's mouth, and she and Goiter hogtied them both and rolled them down a short slope into the cover of thick brush. Next, Andrew made La Fleuvre right the upside-down trunk, open it, and remove all of the contents.

Sure enough, there were two money belts containing a total of 480 dollars.

Goiter began to tremble when he saw the money in Andrew's hands.

Andrew crushed the bills with his fists as he shook them in the air and shouted with glee.

"Take me with you," La Fleuvre insisted as Goiter trained his gun on her.

Instead they gagged her and tied her to a tree behind the thick brush by Vine and the driver.

Andrew and Goiter sat together on the carriage driver's seat. Andrew picked up the leather reigns and held them as if they were mystical Indonesian artifacts.

"We'll disconnect these horses and leave the carriage behind," Andrew said with relish.

"Who is that?" Goiter pointed.

In the distance a figure on horseback approached them.

Andrew took a deep breath. "Do what I say." He glanced behind him to be sure Mr. Vine and the rest remained hidden in the brush.

"They've found us! The gang. They've sent another killer."

"Would you shut up?" Andrew said. "He's coming from the west. Unhitch, or whatever you call it, these horses from the wagon."

The rider appeared more ungainly a fellow than Goiter, but somehow more surefooted. He smiled too much revealing teeth black with tobacco stains. A large Remington hung from his belt. He tipped a weathered brown hat too big for his head and too fashionable for his manner.

Not his hat, thought Andrew.

"Can I assist you gentleman?" The rider's voice sounded higher than Andrew expected and sinister in tone.

"We had an accident." Andrew indicated the open luggage on the ground. "But we're all right now."

"The world is filled with accidents," the rider said. "Like your running into me." His mouth formed an acid grin.

Goiter glanced worriedly at Andrew.

"Do I know you?" Andrew asked.

"Only if you've read the papers," came the answer.

Goiter gasped as the rider's hand fell to his gun and raised it in a blinding fast moment.

A gunshot tore through the air. The rider fell lifeless and heavy to the ground. Goiter turned his head to catch Andrew, cold-eyed, lowering his smoking revolver.

The rider's horse whinnied and pulled back onto its rear legs. Andrew gave it a hard slap with his hat. "I'll take this one. You take one from the coach."

Goiter hunted around for a shovel.

"We have to get out of here," Andrew said. "Help me unhitch these horses."

They left the dead rider where he fell. They threw the saddle pack with the two money belts inside over the back of Andrew's horse and tied it secure. Luck rewarded them in that the stagecoach horses were fairly docile and didn't protest when Goiter struggled to mount one without benefit of stirrups or saddle.

"The doctor doesn't want us? Who cares? We've got money now, and we'll get more. We'll buy you a saddle at the first town we come to. Or maybe we'll steal one!"

Much shouting and moaning followed as Goiter jounced and bobbed along riding bareback behind Andrew. He slid off his horse four times.

The sun lowered on the flat horizon and turned an orange-red, bleeding its colors across the base of the sky. The immense openness of the Platte gave the feeling that anything and nothing was possible.

At a small mud hole while the horses drank Andrew said, "I killed a human being. I could have just wounded him."

"He was going to kill us." Goiter rubbed his sore haunches. His shirt was soaked through with perspiration.

"My face is hot."

"You're excited," Goiter said.

"Excited?" Andrew massaged his forehead with his fingers. "Scared is more like it."

"You're scared that you're excited."

"How do you know?" Andrew asked.

"Killing people makes me feel alive," Goiter answered. "Killing makes me feel like...I'm part of something. If I don't kill someone at least once a month I get sad and lonely and get to feeling like I'm nothing."

Andrew appeared terrified. "That's how I feel about opium and young men."

Goiter took his turn looking terrified. "I guess that's maybe how it is."

"I'm not like that," said Andrew. "Killing is gauche."

"I don't know what 'gauche' means, but you steal money and fight men for no reason. Is that gauche?"

"You're smarter than I thought you were," Andrew said. "But, I'm no killer."

"Anybody is a killer," Goiter said. "That's what my father used to say. All it takes is once."

Goiter watched Andrew with much interest. The fop looked delighted and horrified and pale.

"Finding a true friend is like finding a deenar in the street – very rare," Goiter's father had always said.

As for the perversion, there had been men like Andrew in Prussia, but they were mostly confined to the forest or the royal family and were never seen in an average village.

"Who is this Senator that made you so angry?" Goiter asked Andrew as Andrew mounted his horse.

The expression hardened on Andrew's face. "One thing in private and one thing in public. That's who. A man with a cold heart."

Goiter took a deep breath of prairie air.

Andrew gave his horse a kick and galloped ahead.

8. Revelation at the Dear God River

Black coils of thick clouds drifted toward the wagons.

"Everyone on the horses," John shouted.

"And leave our wagons here?" cried Wife #2. "No!"

"Did you ever see oxen fly?"

They all mounted the horses.

Christian Joseph felt a heaviness in the air and a foreboding as if the whole earth were crouching and waiting for something larger than itself to break down doors and windows and the flat vast prairie beyond. He could smell the rain in the distance. The ground grew more pungent, too, with flowering wild grasses giving off scent as their only weapon against what was coming.

His coat flapped at his sides as he helped Marianne tie down boxes and bags inside their wagon. "What terrible things have you done?" he asked Kelly.

The other boy was struggling with a polished oak-framed mirror, and the leather straps that wouldn't quite reach around it to affix it to the wagon's frame. "You afraid?"

"No. I read books about people who do terrible things."

"Books? Oh, ho ho ho ho! No wonder you are so ridiculous!" Kelly leaned in close and his soft voice was more audible against the increasing rush of the wind outside. "They say I have no feelings," he hissed. "Because of things I've done against my parents."

"Get out! C'mon, get on the horses! We're leaving the wagons here!" shouted Francis Piggott outside the open wagon flaps. The late afternoon sky loomed black with clouds behind Piggott's rough silhouette.

Christian Joseph found it hard to break the stare the two boys held between them, a horrible stare of knowing and not knowing. He let Piggott pull him out of the wagon and set him behind him on one of the strong horses, while Kelly got out without help and rushed off to the horse that Wife #1, Marianne, sat atop and held waiting for him.

Together, almost at once, the forty members of the Mormon emigrant train spurred their horses away from the tornado that grew larger than the rest of the horizon. Christian Joseph held onto Piggott's coat for dear life as the galloping animal beneath them sped them over the uneven ground, discomposing the boy mercilessly. He dared to crane his neck to observe behind them and felt his face grow cold and his eyes tear up when he saw that the tornado would shortly overtake them.

It wasn't the sight of torn clothing flying through the air. It wasn't even the sight of the collie dog whisking by surrounded by cups and tins from one of the train's kitchen lockers. It was the sight of Wife #2 aloft and kicking her legs, her bloomers filled with humid air and the black debris cyclone swirling all around her that truly scared the beejeesus out of Dr. Gray.

She whipped her horse with the belt she had removed from her pants. Pieces of wagons they had left behind sailed above them velocities faster than that of the galloping terrified horse. A hand mirror zoomed by. A tin chamber pot rose over the horse's head and then zoomed straight up and out of sight entirely. Chickens and bonnets and leather pouches and pans jumbled about and clattered and shattered until Dr. Gray let go of a moan of pure horror.

The monstrous cyclone spun mere yards away, and in one desperate final attempt at escape, Dr. Gray gave the bridle a Herculean yank to the right, and the horse avoided stumbling and violently collapsing to the earth by inches.

He was a fine steed despite the force of the wind behind them, and Dr. Gray was able to guide him to a part of the nearby prairie that waited breathlessly for the leviathan winds to pass.

On a small rise, she pulled back on the reigns with aching fingers and turned the horse to face the plain. The cyclone was a tangle of black hair on the horizon, large and angry, but moving away to the south. Behind it lay the wrecks of many of the wagons from the Mormon train. Oddly, some of the wagons remained intact, but not many. The row of little hills stretched for some distance, and the doctor could see the figures of five other horses with their riders, several of them waving and calling out, their voices muted by distance and air currents. The doctor held her hand to her forehead to shade her eyes and wondered if Christian Joseph sat atop one of the safe steeds.

She observed a few children running with their mothers without horses toward the riders. As the doctor scanned the distance in the dusk of the coming evening she could barely make out many figures across the plain. Some were getting to their feet, others hunched over the motionless figures of their comrades. From somewhere came the sound of crying.

"Well, well!" A woman's strained voice from behind her startled even the horse.

The doctor glanced quickly around. Marianne stood before her, her yellow dress in tatters and smeared with dust. Her hair uncoiled and puffed up in primeval disarray. "Marianne."

"Have you seen John?"

The doctor answered no. "Have you seen Christian Joseph?"

"No. I almost didn't recognize you."

Something made the doctor touch her chin.

As a small tremor ran through her, Marianne asked, "Find time for a shave?"

The doctor felt patches of remaining glue. The beard was gone!

The look Marianne gave her unnerved her. Behind her the sky retained swirls of gray and charcoal blending to a dim night blue. With a tone of condemnation, Marianne informed her, "I'm going to look for my husband. I'll tell your boy where you are if I see him." She marched resolutely down the hillside.

Without the hot beard, the air felt transcendent on the doctor's face. She ran her fingertips along her cheeks. A terrible sadness passed through her. How she wanted her face out in the open, free of the pathetic disguise. She felt complete in that moment, seated atop a horse out in the vast open prairie, wearing a man's clothes. She allowed the moments of complete freedom to pass one after the other. She luxuriated in them.

The cyclone receded farther and became smaller on the horizon. The doctor gave her horse a gentle kick and descended the hill farther to the north than Marianne. She thought of offering her a ride so as to make an ally of her, to prevent the disastrous confrontations that were sure to come, but something prevented her. She decided to table that worry for now. Even with the understanding that her trip with the wagon train had ended.

Many of the emigrants would be injured and in need of her attention. And there was the boy. The boy was the only "friend" the doctor
had. Before they could escape the punishment for their deception, she
would have to find the boy.

Christian Joseph opened his eyes. He was lying flat on his back, and
the sky above him became gray-blue streaked with wisps of brown. For
a moment, he did not make an effort to move. The wind whistled over
him, and he came to understand that the tornado had passed and the
air behind it was still roiling.

He remembered being airborne, for how long he didn't know.
He had been thrown violently sidewise, up and then down hard. He
had felt dust and grass and smelled fresh soil filling the atmosphere
blinding him while he kicked his feet in search of ground.

Piggott and the horse had been knocked over together. The horse
had whinnied, and Piggott had reached to grab Christian and hold
him fast, but not in time.

Christian craned his head but saw only the lonely prairie surrounding him.

With a moan, he sat up. It occurred to him he might be injured, but
a quick check turned up nothing but bruises, torn pant legs, and cuts
on his hands.

Strange sensations of exhilaration and fear filled him. Was that
how Andrew felt after a fight or when he shot a gun? Was that the
intoxication of life?

How momentary! What did a person do during the long endless
"in-between" times? How could anyone be satisfied when true excitement happened so rarely?

The boy got to his feet, felt dizzy, and sat back down. The exhilaration he had felt from surviving being airborne was similar to what

he had felt waiting for the train at his Adventure Spot back in Ohio. A thrilling window had been opened, no matter how briefly.

Only now it had slammed shut again. Traveling west was exciting, yes, but too often it had become uncomfortable and disappointing.

Christian Joseph was used to carpeted parlors, clean sheets in a stationary bed, and the smell of new books. Adventure was something to be written down, reflected upon, chronicled, and even made up altogether. Day to day, he realized, he was not cut out for it. He loved the moments of intoxication, but the "in-between" times were too uncomfortable.

He missed his mother's bread pudding. He missed his bedroom with the old block children's toys. Sure, he knew he was becoming a man, but he wasn't ready just yet. He was only thirteen. Perhaps, he wondered, that was why he looked up to Andrew Bolding. Andrew could be all the things Christian Joseph imagined were worthwhile, without Christian Joseph actually having to do any of those things.

And wasn't that what writing and reading were all about?

Or maybe he just missed his idol? What fun was flying through the air in a tornado without someone to share it all with?

The air around him grew eerily still and the funnel cloud tore far off to the east. Visible on the huge flat horizon in the dimming light were cattle, chickens, boxes, and several figures like himself walking alone or in pairs, calling out. He wondered about Dr. Gray and the Mormon family, Mr. Piggott and even the hateful Kelly.

He thought briefly about running away, even scanned the southern horizon where Mexico was, but an image of himself being eaten by buzzards or enslaved and tortured by Indians immediately leapt into his mind. Too many penny novels, as his mother used to say.

Feeling confused, he began to walk slowly toward the others and their shouts and calls. Andrew Bolding had clarity of purpose. Maybe that was what appealed to Christian Joseph. Andrew seemed to know what was what in the world and wasn't afraid of it.

More than anything Christian Joseph wanted to find his hero again.

"He's a woman!" Marianne exclaimed as the family huddled around her. The wagons and their families had slowly regrouped as the sun set, and those that still had horses and wagons that functioned had gathered near the eastern bank of the Dear God River.

"This fraud is a woman. What kind of beard can be ripped off by the wind?"

John had sustained only cuts and gashes to his hands from being torn from the reigns of his horse. Francis Piggott crouched nearby with John's other two wives.

"That's fine!" said Wife #2. "How are we to make it to Utah without a wagon? Shall we ride wild ducks? Shall we wait for another twister and hope it carries us to where we want to go?"

"That's enough!" John rose to his feet. "What did happen to your beard, sir?" he asked.

Dr. Gray tipped her hat low over her face, averting her eyes from those of John. After a moment, she slowly stood up and dusted her pants with her hands. She removed her hat and walked to the center of the distraught Mormons. "It is true. I am a woman."

Only the wind could be heard, still buffeting the low shrubs of the plain.

"A woman...doctor?" John asked.

"I am one of the best in the profession," Dr. Gray said. "Have I not healed all who were sick on this ill-fated trip?"

Kelly stepped in from the ring of alarmed family members. Both his bare knees were scraped bloody. "I'm not surprised. Where is the pasty boy? He's probably a woman, too."

"What is so wrong with being a woman?" Dr. Gray asked.

"Nothing," Wife #2 said, "if a woman knows her place."

"What place is that?" Dr. Gray asked.

"You are an aberration," Marianne muttered.

John stepped forward, face flushed and teeth set. "She is a woman! A woman who is a fine doctor, and we are lucky to have her. We are blessed to have this woman amongst us! She has been sent to us! What does it matter what sex she be? She made an able man, equal to many."

Dr. Gray felt her breath catch in her throat.

"Did she not heal you when you had the rash all over your face?" John asked.

Wife #2 did not agree, but everyone knew John was right.

"Did she not give you medicine when you could not stop going to the bathroom and the wagons had to wait –?"

"Yes, she did!" interrupted Kelly, embarrassed.

"We had no doctor," John went on. "This woman came to us with the best doctor training anyone could have."

"It is a sin to dress as a man," Marianne hissed from her place on the ground.

"We are emigrating to a new land," John said. "Will you not go as a woman now that God's vengeance has passed?" he asked Dr. Gray. "We are all cleansed of our sins this night."

"What sins?" Wife #2 said.

"Need I list them all? Everyone here, including myself has sinned. You, Wife #2, you have danced with animals."

"I was helping the ox get to its feet."

"While humming?"

An uncomfortable silence followed.

"Kelly. Need I list all that you have done?"

Dr. Gray felt dizzy, perhaps a form of shock from so narrowly escaping the tornado combined with being unmasked before everyone with no excuse, no explanation. To escape the feelings of dread at being discovered, she dwelt on a sense of pride at handling her horse so well as to escape a monster prairie cyclone. "Where is my ward?"

"How do we know he is your ward?" asked Kelly. "If you were not a man, how can we believe anything you have said?"

"What do you think he is, a talking sausage? He is a person. He is my responsibility." Dr. Gray removed her hat, shook off the dust, and returned it to her head to shade her eyes as she surveyed the exhaustingly immense landscape.

"In the morning we will go about finding all of our wagons and livestock," John told the others. "We must reassemble our outfit as soon as possible."

"And bury the dead," Marianne added.

Indeed, there was much to be done. They built a fire with flint John carried and helped Marianne into one of the few remaining wagons to rest.

"What strength you have," John told Dr. Gray, when they were alone. "To go about as a man."

"Thank you, John. But I can't stay with you. I can't wear a giant bonnet and one of those tents they call dresses. Once I find Christian Joseph, we will go our own way."

"Without a horse or provisions?"

"At the first fort we come to you can drop us off."

"Won't you stay with me?" John asked. "I would be honored if you would become one of my wives."

Dr. Gray sighed. There was no sign of Christian Joseph. Night was coming fast. She turned to face the tall Mormon. "Thank you for the offer, John. My future is in Utopia. That's where I'm headed. Not Salt Lake City. Besides, don't you have enough wives?"

John appeared almost bashful at the mention of too many wives. "The more wives I have, the lonelier I become."

Far in the distance in the last remaining light near a rocky outcrop above the river, Dr. Gray discerned a boy waving a book. She had never wanted a child, but she found herself flooded with joy that the boy was all right.

"I'll take you to him," John said. He put his thumb and forefinger to his mouth and whistled for Kelly to bring a horse.

And for a moment, Dr. Gray wondered if she didn't have something in common with the women who were John's wives. Before the thought could become very clear, she shook it from her mind.

9. Arrival

After several weeks of riding stolen horses, Andrew and Goiter arrived at Utopia Valley. It was late in the afternoon of June tenth. Visible was a small settlement with smoke curling from a chimney, obviously "the town." To the south stretched a huge expanse of fenced-in land and livestock and a gothic-spired enormous house set far back toward the foothills. The Wunderfahrt Ranch!

As they rode toward the overly elaborate iron gate at the front of the ranch house grounds, Goiter asked, "Why don't we just live off the money from the stagecoach?"

"I was an accountant. One of the first rules of money is to *save it*. Plus, someone is bound to identify those jewels or the cash somewhere along the line. We'll blend in at this job."

Goiter frowned. "Give me some," he asked half-heartedly.

Andrew ignored him. He felt fatigue building. All the days with Goiter and his anxieties and lack of poise, not to mention the heat and sweat of riding horses across a prairie, had taken their toll. And he had lost his best friend.

The front gate sported two gargoyles; one perched on either side atop stone pedestals.

Andrew ran his teeth over his bottom lip. Something shouted out to him from deep inside that he was making another in a long list of wrong decisions for his life. But it no longer mattered. Who cared, after all? He thought of the heat that ran through him whenever he fired his gun.

"You're not on the list." A roughneck with a notebook looked them up and down. They stood in front of a large barn just inside the front gate.

Behind the roughneck, far back on the porch to the great house, Andrew could make out a woman wearing a long black dress speaking with several other ranch hands. They all turned and scrutinized Andrew and Goiter.

"We wouldn't be on the list because we're here to help out. Goiter here is a professional murderer, and I am Andrew Bolding."

"Well, Bolding, we don't need nobody else."

"That's ridiculous! Terrorizing a whole valley takes all the men you can get!"

"What I mean is," the roughneck said, "we ain't payin' nobody else."

Goiter shot Andrew a nasty glance.

"Who do you have on that paper now?" Andrew asked.

The roughneck spit into the dirt near a hitching post and checked his list. "Fritters McDougal, Blanchard Jones, Bastard Ass..."

"Bastard Ass?"

"...Roger Fent, Cancer, Doug...ain't got no last name...Look, I ain't readin' any more of this list. I got better things to do."

"Where is Wunderfatt?"

"Wunderfahrt? Mr. Lucien Wunderfahrt?"

"Yes," Andrew said.

"He won't speak to you."

There was a whistle from one of the men back at the house. The roughneck instructed Andrew and Goiter to wait.

Goiter crossed his arms and squinted worriedly about the premises. If ever there were a place for another assassin to jump out and shoot them, here it was.

"Why did you tell him I'm a professional killer?" he asked Andrew. "The gang is bound to find me here if everyone knows I'm a killer just arrived."

"They're all killers here," Andrew said and then cleared his throat. "I mean, we can't tell them we're peace lovers, now can we?"

Five minutes passed.

Gretchen Wunderfahrt shielded her eyes from the sun as she hurried from the porch out to the barn. A breeze blew the black lace that she wore tied in her hair. She wasn't a beauty. "We got us a true-to-life gunslinger here," she said with amusement once she had joined them. "And this is his number one man, an escaped lunatic from the Asylum."

"That's not tr—"

Andrew elbowed Goiter in the stomach. "That's right. This is my lunatic assistant. He escaped from the nuthouse. I taught him how to dress himself."

Goiter scowled at the ground.

"How did you hear of us?" Andrew asked.

"The prairie has ears," Gretchen answered. "I got some nasty men already hired, and I don't need just any idiot signin' up just so's they can get drunk, ride around hollerin', and then collect a paycheck. But I heard about what you did at the stagecoach, and some more..."

"What more?"

Gretchen placed her hands on her hips. The sun hit her black dress revealing the frayed pattern, come from a certain indifference to social appearance. "You've got a different look to you." She ran her tongue along her bottom lip.

"So do you, ma'am." The right corner of Andrew's mouth lifted just a bit and his eyes narrowed.

Goiter felt faint. The sly look that Andrew gave to Gretchen was enough to seize up anyone's stomach. Still, at least he would get the job. At least he'd be paid.

"The soft walkers across the river might go for you if you're not careful," Gretchen went on.

"My mind will be on this side of the river, ma'am," Andrew said.

Gretchen chewed her lower lip. There was a brightness in her eyes. Goiter caught her noticing the black painted nails on Andrew's fingers. "Gunslingers are a different breed," she said with authority. "Losers and drunks the lot of them, but a different breed, still. I wouldn't spend a moment with any of them."

"Neither would I, ma'am. Where do we throw our bags?"

"Jimmy! Show them the bunkhouse and tell them the rules. Tonight they'll go with you into town. Get their clothes in the laundry tomorrow. And put them on the damn list!"

Utopia lay before them in the center of a valley too beautiful for its own good. A gentle mid-June breeze rustled the hair back from Christian Joseph's face. At last, after weeks of traveling with the doctor and a Mormon guide John had provided for them, they had arrived. The guide had gone on to Salt Lake City after depositing them within walking distance of the town. From their vantage point atop the crest of a large plateau, looking west, they could see the Utopia River and the twenty or thirty buildings of the town where the river bent sharply on its journey south.

Christian Joseph glanced up at Dr. Gray. The backup beard retained a "fresh-out-of-the-box" look. The doctor held her hat in place with her left hand and appeared to be taking the whole valley in like a table spread at Thanksgiving. "Looks peaceful enough," the doctor surmised.

The doctor pulled the brim of her hat low over her forehead to shield her from the brilliant sunlight. They filed down the trail to the Utopia Valley below.

They reached the town by 5:30. The Screaming Lilly Saloon stood opposite Babe's Mercantile and Medicine, a rickety structure with windows shielding stacks of tins and bottles with lozenge colored labels. White lace curtains pulled back revealed the displays.

The sound of a piano floated from the Screaming Lilly, and beyond the low saloon doors, Dr. Gray could only make out the silhouettes of one or two men. Flume Street was dusty and rutted.

A post office and a dry goods store pressed close together. The rest of the buildings stood unmarked, private homes and storage buildings perhaps. On a crooked board was scrawled in charcoal "mining stakes and claims."

"We'll finally get you back into school," Dr. Gray said as they walked slowly down the street. She felt a profound dismay. After all that she had heard, the town appeared decidedly average. No gold pavement. No smiling laughing crowds. Just a regular town from streetside.

She hated to be reminded dreams rarely matched cold reality.

They entered Babe's Mercantile and Medicine. A little bell on the inside door jamb announced them.

"Mama! You got cust'mers!" shouted a boy, perhaps eleven or twelve, dressed in only a long faded blue nightshirt. His messy blond-white hair cut medium length framed his face, and he tinkered with some polished stones arranged in geometric shapes on the plank floor.

"Name's Babe. What can I do you for?" asked a sturdy woman of the type Dr. Gray was familiar with back in New York.

"I'm the new doctor. I've got this letter."

"Oh?" A faint look of surprise crossed the woman's face. "Garrison! Why ain't you dressed? What is wrong with you? Get some pants on and a shirt or you won't have any dinner!"

"I am too sick! I've got anemic dysentery! I won't get dressed. I won't!"

Christian Joseph frowned. Even the evil Mormon boy had been better behaved.

"This is Garrison," Babe said. "He makes things up so's people will look at him." The woman stuck out her right hand, and the doctor shook it. "Glad to know ya! We need a doctor 'round here. What's you dressed up like a man, fer?"

The doctor frowned.

"I've seen it before. You're the first Black woman I seen do it, though. We all gotta stick together, right?" Babe gave the doctor a nod. "I was told by the mayor before he died to keep my eye out for you."

"What happened to him?" the doctor asked.

"Killed himself over at the Wunderfahrt Ranch, if you believe that story. There's a room for you and your boy upstairs."

"Not my room! They can't have my room!" Garrison shouted.

"Not your room!" Babe shot back. "Honestly!" She leaned in close to Dr. Gray. "His parents left him here. Thought he was 'funny' if you know what I mean. Just left the poor kid. Now he's mine."

Babe showed Dr. Gray and Christian to a large room upstairs with a window facing the street and the saloon. The room was plain but comfortable with purple drapes and kerosene lamps sporting turquoise-colored holders.

"We got a list of people that want to see you, Dr. Gray," Babe said when the doctor had seated herself atop the large bed and began to unlace her boots. Christian Joseph sat on a stool by a little wood stove. The air was clean and pungent with the smell of sagebrush. "I'll get Garrison to bring up a cot for the youngin'. There's a town meetin' tomorrow night. I'll take ya, you can meet everyone and see what we're up against."

Dr. Gray sighed, and took off her hat. "Thank you, Babe. A friend of mine is expected to join us. His name is Andrew Bolding. Will you tell me if anyone hears from him?"

"Sure will." Babe winked. She left them there and closed the door on her way out.

"We did it! We're here!" Dr. Gray exclaimed, and she threw herself back on the bed with her arms outstretched. "I've got a job!"

"Are you crying?" asked Christian Joseph.

"I'm all right." The doctor ran her hand over her collar. "This is Utopia. If it's anything like I've heard, then my life may be completely different."

Christian Joseph got up and came over to the bed. He sat delicately on the edge near the doctor's knees. "Babe said I was your boy. I'm not your boy."

The doctor became still. Without sitting up, she said, "We should talk about you. You can stay with me until we figure everything out. See what this place is really like. Don't worry, Christian, you're safe with me."

Christian Joseph allowed himself to lie back on the bed next to the doctor and stare up at the paisley canopy with dangly things hanging from the fringes.

"What happened to Dr. Childs? The man who wrote to me?" Dr. Gray asked that night at dinner. They were seated in a room back from the mercantile storefront, a room Babe used as a kitchen and pantry.

Babe ladled out huge scoops of mashed potatoes from a pot onto a plate and then handed it firmly to Garrison, who had remained in his nightshirt since the afternoon. "The Wunderfahrts shot him," Babe said. "Peas?"

"Yes, please. Shot him?"

"The Wunderfahrts. The ranchers. Oh, you'll find out all about it tomorrow. They threatened me, too, but nobody tells Babe Winters what she can or can't do."

Garrison rolled his eyes in pained agreement.

"In fact," Babe went on, ladling out spoonfuls of peas for each plate, "they tell me it's dangerous to live in town like I do, to live on my own storefront property. I'm not afraid. Utopia is my home. Nobody can take away my home."

When the doctor asked where Babe's home was before Utopia, she answered, "Sad little place in Maryland. I wore pants, and nobody talked to me. One day I met a woman passing through on her way here. I was packed in five minutes."

The venison was delicious. It was seasoned with garlic pepper and garnished with pieces of orange.

Dr. Gray and Christian Joseph ate with gusto. Garrison laid his fork down. "I have Corporeal Dislexiosis. I can't eat. I may die. I can't feel my neck."

Babe grinned while she chewed. "Garrison is a real ham. I've taken to him. Never thought I'd be a mama. Never been with a man. But here we are, a little family." She tousled his rat's nest of hair. "Maybe you'll perform one of your 'dramas' for the new doctor and her boy after we have our coffee, huh, Gary?"

Garrison scowled and looked askance at the ceiling. "Don't you call me Gary! How I loathe to be called Gary!" He pushed back his chair, stood up without looking at anyone, and beckoning to the stairway with his right hand, he took two steps toward it.

"Don't move!" Babe said. "Sit down and eat this food I busted my backside to make for you, and then you'll clean up all these dishes, or I'll smack you."

Garrison hesitated in his dramatic gesture. All at once, he sat back down and began to eat.

There was a little sitting room upstairs facing south. The dinner party gathered there for dessert and to see Garrison perform. Through the window flickered the lights of the distant Wunderfahrt Ranch.

Babe served strawberry and chocolate petit forts and coffee for herself and Dr. Gray. Christian Joseph sat happily on an old French divan.

Surrounded by ten lit candles strategically spaced around the room, Garrison, still dressed only in his nightshirt, performed one of his "little dramas." This one was entitled, as Babe revealed before he began, "The Sirens of Fear Valley."

This couldn't be any better, thought Christian Joseph. *I wish I'd thought of that title.* And then Christian dropped his petit fort as Garrison let loose a heart stopping wail and fell to his knees where he delivered a long monologue as the lead siren who was afraid everyone was dead.

The town meeting the next evening was held at the Bear Rocks Silver Mine in an underground cavern with secure solid walls and a thick stone roof. Babe drove the doctor, Garrison, and Christian in her wagon down the dirt road the five miles from town to the mines.

"They can't do anything to anyone in the cavern," Babe said. "They can't burn it down or shoot through it. We post a few guards along the rocks to watch out for the Wunderfahrt boys."

Garrison wore canvas pants and a factory-made gray wool shirt. He sat sulkily next to Christian Joseph in the back of the wagon as it rumbled along.

Dr. Gray remained dressed as a man in her freshly laundered shirt, jacket, and breeches. After so long, the clothes felt right. She realized dressing as a woman would be the awkward action to take. Without the damned beard, she liked how the clothes felt on her. She realized her phony man's voice and posture were the things she could let go of. *But what would take their place?* she wondered.

She hadn't known about Utopia being threatened. The stories told in New York didn't mention the Wunderfahrts and their men. *Kind of defeats the whole purpose of naming the place "Utopia."* she thought. *The town was supposed to be free of the hatred that exists everywhere else.*

Horses and wagons stood tied to posts along the mine entrance. Several small gas lanterns sent flickering squares of light over the hard packed soil of the quarry.

The air smelled of dry dust.

The thrill of the new rekindled inside of Christian Joseph. An actual cave! Two men greeted them outside, both large and both with hairy forearms and hair poking out where their collars were open. "Welcome to the Bear Rock Mines." One tipped an imaginary hat to Christian Joseph.

"We call them the Hairy Bears," Babe said.

Inside, the cavern was like nothing Christian had ever seen. Rugs lined the floor. Apparently, the bears used this front cavern as an office space, rather than build structures of wood outside. Neatly stacked papers sat on several desks. Gas lamps hung on rock walls with dark soot stains spattered above their flames. Shadows danced on the ceiling. Several tunnels led from the cavern into dark passageways.

"The main entrance where they have their rails and dirty machinery is on the other side of this hill," Babe explained.

The cavern dwarfed the visitors. Perhaps twenty folding canvas stools faced a wall with a small oil painting of James "Grizzly" McBay. There were large loose boulders in the back. Approximately thirty townspeople talked in low echoing voices.

Several small children ran about laughing and playing "tag." Two collie dogs chased them and jumped as they played. Some of the women wore long skirts and bonnets, but most wore pants and boots. The bears wore dirty smocks and trousers no doubt the result of a hard day's work underground. The other men present were of varying ages. Some were from the Screaming Lilly Saloon.

After some time, a man with a full beard stood before the painting and motioned for everyone to sit on stools and boulders and for the meeting to begin.

"Hello, I'm Gorgeous Fenster," the man said. "I run this mine. As you know our sheriff ran off after the doctor was killed. In addition, many of us have been offered large sums of money for our ranches. I, myself, have been offered five thousand dollars for this mining operation. I declined."

There was a murmur from the audience.

"We have lost some of our residents due to intimidation by the Wunderfahrt gang," Fenster went on, "But tonight we have a new neighbor to welcome. We have at last, a new doctor: Dr. Troy Gray."

Unanimous applause echoed in the cave. Heads turned, and Dr. Gray felt compelled to stand and nod her head once in recognition of the attention. But it was more than that. She wasn't alone in a sea of white faces. Instead, there were people of all kinds of backgrounds.

"All the way from New York City!" Gorgeous Fenster added. More applause and cheering followed. Several people stood up and headed to where the doctor remained seated in the back.

"Now, leave that doctor alone until after the meeting."

A man wearing nothing but a sheet draped around his waist stood up. "I'm Josh Breeze, and as everyone knows, I run the nude dentistry office on Flume Street. We've already lost most of the Water Mill women. They took the money the Wunderfahrts offered, and they went to Montana. I will not sell out. This is Utopia! If someone offers me a small fortune, all for the good, except where will I run naked and free, painting oils of male prostitutes? Boston? No! We must keep this valley. We must fight the Wunderfahrts!"

Josh Breeze continued prompted by substantial cheering and applause. "Those Wunderfahrt roughnecks hang round down by the Mill Stream and catcall me every morning. "Look, it's a giant shrimp walking around! A giant pink shrimp! And they whistle and call, hey baby! And, do a dance! And all manner of sayings!"

"Well, if you didn't run around nude maybe they'd leave you alone! Hello, everyone. I'm Virginia Soakes." A wiry woman stood near the boulders in the back. She had been seated quite close to Dr. Gray and Christian Joseph. "I run the pawn shop, and I'm pretty sure I've met every last one of you already. Josh, I was the one who lent you the salve to put on that rash you contracted from the spring foliage, remember? We've been friends ever since. We read the Torah together nude, for Godsakes! I didn't move here to be part of a war. I moved here to finally get some peace. To finally be left alone!"

"Josh isn't provoking those Wunderfahrts." Babe stood up an arm's length from Virginia. "Hello, everyone, Babe Winters here. Virginia and me was one of the first women ever to move to Utopia back in '51. We split up because of her need to be alone and because she eats with her mouth open which I just can't stand. We are all being provoked. Those Wunderfahrt boys let two wild pigs and a ferret loose in your pawn shop last month, Virginia. Have you forgotten? And what about the threats they make to burn down the Screaming Lilly and burn all of our houses? That's what this meeting is about. Those Wunderfahrts are organized. That's what we've got to do. Organize!"

"Hold on, Babe." A man wearing a wool tunic and sandals stood up. "You all know me," he addressed the group. "I'm Genius Ward. I grow opium for Babe's medicine shop. I love Utopia just like the rest of you do, but if we fight and if we organize, many of us will be killed along with our children. I've seen enough sorrow, and so have you."

"What will you do, then?" Babe shot back. "You live with a white man. If the Wunderfahrts give you money to leave, where will you two men go and live without fear? We all know there have been other communities like Utopia that have tried to survive and were destroyed."

"What we need," Gorgeous Fenster said, taking back control of the meeting, "is law enforcement."

"The Wunderfahrts will crush them," Josh said. "They killed the doctor. They killed the mayor –"

"Killed himself," Gorgeous Fenster said, "...was the official story. We have no mayor. And the Wunderfahrts will rig any election. We can't call territorial government for help because our 'commune' as they call us, is considered an aberration in the site of –"

"God. Yes, we all know that," Babe interrupted.

"They cain't invade us because we have the most popular brothel in the whole west." Poor Montgomery stood up. He was willowy, handsome, and dressed like a ranch hand. "I agree with Babe and Josh. We must organize. And what you people forgets is we have an advantage. Some of those Wunderfahrts are regulars at the Screaming Lilly.

"The reason they hate us is because we got what they want. Real freedom. They skulk around and chase us behind closed doors, but they don't got the guts to admit we have what they want: Freedom, whether they are like us or not. Real freedom like what this whole country is supposed to be about."

The room erupted in applause all at once. Surprise lit Poor Montgomery's face.

"We won't sell our mine." Gorgeous Fenster spoke when the cheering had subsided. "We dug this mine. We have children that we are raising here."

"Whores and miners aren't enough," Babe said. "If more of the rest of us take the money and leave like the Water Mill women, we'll still lose Utopia."

"And if we stay," Gorgeous Fenster said. "We risk our lives at the hands of those murderers."

"Like the sheriff. They'll kill us all or burn down our houses."

Dr. Gray hung her head low. After months of saving money and planning and then risking life and limb traveling through the wilderness, it seemed everything had been in vain.

10. TENSION ON THE PRAIRIE

Several of the Wunderfahrt ranch hands smoked hand-rolled cigarettes behind the barn. "I was told we have to ratchet it up a notch
on those soft-walkers." Tom spit tobacco on the ground. "We're supposed to terrorize 'em."

"I ain't never terrorized no one before," Scritch said.

"Well, yah, you have been. That's what breakin' their windows and
stealin' pigs is. Only now we got to threaten their lives and burn down
their houses."

Goiter watched the proceedings with alarm. A man in the back
shadows, dressed shabbily, glared at him. Goiter recognized the round
face but knew not from where.

"I had a job in California scarin' miners off their claims. You dress
up like a demon at night and run through their camp shootin' and
steal one of their kids. Always works," Tom said.

"Set fire to their crops. Nothin' like burnin' onions," Scritch said.
"Just make sure you do it right. Friend of mine set crops on fire all
around him and then burned to death in the middle."

"What about you?" the man glaring at Goiter asked. "You ever terrorized?"

Goiter cleared his throat.

"Sure, look at 'im," said Tom. "Just walkin' around would terrorize anyone."

Goiter frowned. "In New York –"

Andrew elbowed him.

"Er...uh...in Prussia where I'm from I used to tie the chickens together."

Puzzled expressions gave way to howling laughter.

"I kill people," Goiter added.

"Yeah? Who did you kill lately?"

"Andrew here killed a man just two weeks ago –"

Again, Andrew elbowed him.

"Although, I'm not sure," Goiter added.

"You two are strange heifers, that's for sure," Tom said.

"I'll say they are," the man glaring at Goiter chimed in. "I saw the fancy one struttin' around for ol' Gretchen there. He thinks he's somethin' special. What's he got painted around his eyes? Looks bookish to me."

"Maybe so," Scritch said. "Maybe I should beat the tar out of him. Gretchen likes me best."

Low laughter.

Goiter noticed Andrew's face flush. "Maybe I'll wallop your sorry ass so you can't walk," Andrew said.

More laughter, but not from Scritch.

"That's funny," the man glaring at Goiter said. "You look like a fancy pants accountant to me."

Goiter noticed Andrew's head jerk to discern the man in the gloom. "No. Not me. Don't know how to read and write."

"Really?" the man laughed.

Goiter felt a shiver crawl up his back as he remembered who the man was. His name was Charles, and he had worked as a pickpocket and a spy back in New York in the gang.

It was only a short matter of time, worried Goiter, before the gang knew where he was and whoever they had sent out after him to finish them off would arrive in Utopia.

11. Olga Red Bootstragen

The schoolmarm for Utopia was the tallest woman Christian Joseph had ever seen. "So, you want to hear the history of our town?" The woman put her hands on her hips. "I can help you be a writer, you know. Sit down."

Christian Joseph took a seat in one of the few attached-to-the-desk chairs. The little room had large windows and a beautiful green play yard outside with a swing and teeter-totter. "So few children in my class want to be writers." Olga Red Bootstragen sighed once. She sat opposite Christian Joseph behind her desk and put her feet up so that her bloomers were just visible above her red boots. "You see, little boy, Utopia isn't really a proper town. Originally all Utopia was was this beautiful valley and the river that cuts through the middle. Then, in 1840, they discovered silver in that Bear Mine. Some old man from Missouri named Smiley. He brought all his mountain man friends. The second thing that happened that was important was the stage and freight line put in a relay post, that meant a place where you could get drinks as well as horses, and well, it gained a reputation. That's what started it all."

"A reputation?"

"Yes, where men could meet men, and women could meet women, and men can dress the way I do, and well, just any taste really that involved consenting adults. I shouldn't tell you any more than that."

Christian Joseph nodded to show he understood and jotted something down on his notepad.

"A saddle shop opened and then a blacksmith salon. Imagine, calling your blacksmith store a 'salon.' But, that's what Petey Schuster called it. He was from New York and had been to Paris so he knew all about art. A few houses were built and then the school. Homesteaders heard about the unusual population here, and farms and the water mill were set up."

"What about the Wunderfahrts?" Christian Joseph asked.

Olga Red Bootstragen glanced out the window at the field outside. She squinted as if in serious thought. "Old Man Wunderfahrt is a rancher and owns the range rights to this entire valley. Was nice enough until the homesteaders started getting in his way. You can find a lot of his cowboys at the Screaming Lilly on a hot afternoon or on a Saturday night, or at Babe's Mercantile and Medicine. Used to get along. Not no more. Not no more."

"Why?"

"Wunderfahrt's got a big contract, and he wants back his valley. I think also, he doesn't like us much, the way we behave in Utopia. The nearest marshall is one hundred miles from here, and our sheriff abandoned us."

Christian Joseph felt a wave of sadness wash over him, a shiver of despair. He didn't know quite why, but perhaps, he thought, it was the same feeling he got when he remembered what it was like to be controlled by his father and his father's church. The way starched short pants felt against his legs and how laughter was forbidden at the dinner table.

Olga Red Bootstragen smiled, revealing very white straight teeth. "You really are a writer! Look at the notes you are taking. I am so happy to have you in my school, Christian Joseph."

"When did you come to Utopia?"

"Last Fourth of July. My wife brought me out here from Chicago."

"Wife?" Christian Joseph said.

"Yes, boy. I am a man. I like women. But I wear women's clothes in public sometimes. There is nothing wrong with that."

Christian Joseph nodded his head slowly in agreement. "I've never met anyone like you."

"That you know of..." Olga said. "You know, there are all different ways of dressing and being."

Christian thought of Dr. Gray.

"There always has been. The world today refuses to understand. Does my talking about this bother you?"

"No. I like interesting people. It's just my family is religious—" Christian said.

Olga put his right palm up. "Say no more. In Chicago they'd hunt men like me down. See this scar?" Olga pulled at his collar revealing a dark scar near his shoulder. "Stabbed just walking down the street. I was wearing a dress. My wife. She died..." Olga Red Bootstragen cleared his throat. "She died last November. Died suddenly while eating my pot roast. Doctor was far away. They said it was her heart. So, it was me that insisted we bring a doctor of our own to Utopia."

There was no hospital, and there were no medical facilities, so Thursday morning, Dr. Gray set up her office in the back room of Babe's Mercantile and Medicine Shop.

"I will contract dyspepsia!" Garrison protested, when he was instructed to clear out the supply boxes filled with new canvas, fresh tinctures laced with opium, coils of rope, and countless sundry odds and ends.

Dr. Gray (still dressed as a man) rolled up her white sleeves, squatted with bent knees, and said, "You don't contract dyspepsia."

Garrison frowned.

At least he has his clothes on today, thought the doctor. *The boy isn't half-bad*. They worked in silence for a while.

When the doctor asked him how old he was, Garrison replied "twelve." And then he blurted, "I don't like it here. I want to go to New York."

The doctor asked him what for and the boy answered, "To become a great actor." He swept dirt off the floor with a straw bristled broom. "I don't like the west. I don't like Utopia."

"Maybe Utopia needs a theater," Dr. Gray said. "New York is no place for a boy all alone."

"A theater? Here?" Garrison stopped sweeping. The thought appeared to be new to him. "How awful to do all the work yourself!" he exclaimed.

"If you want something bad enough…"

There was a rap on the door to the little room. Garrison opened it. Outside was a line of three people. Two men from the Screaming Lilly and one of the relocated Water Mill women.

"See?" Dr. Gray told the boy. "They line up when you have something they want."

Later that morning, a man wearing a brown buttoned shirt and a dusty black top hat stepped in front of one of the Water Mill women, taking the first place in line. He was elderly, but not infirm. There was a square set to his jaw. The others in line wore varying expressions of disdain and apprehension.

"You must see me first," the man told the doctor. "I am Lucien Wunderfahrt."

"You must wait your turn in line," Dr. Gray said.

The others waiting behind him wore expressions of discomfort.

"I'll go first," Lucien Wunderfahrt said with the tone one used to calm an infant. "Does anyone object?" he asked the others in line.

Everyone nodded no.

Dr. Gray hesitated and, picking up on the submission exuded from the others in line, let him in and closed the door.

"A Black doctor?" Lucien looked the doctor up and down like he might a new wagon.

"What brings you to see me?" Dr. Gray asked.

Lucien Wunderfahrt did not sit down. Instead he walked the perimeter of the bare room and inspected the woodwork. "I own this valley, doctor." He glanced with discernment, waited for a reaction, got none, and continued his inspection. "That means I own you." He turned to face the doctor and developed the most reptilian smile. "Welcome to Utopia." He extended his right hand.

Dr. Gray noticed the prominent liver spot before clasping hands and shaking. She could feel Lucien gripping her hand with effort to create a firm grip.

"I like a doctor with a firm grip," Lucien said when they had let go. He sat down in the chair facing the doctor's little desk. "When you get a call from me to come to my ranch, you will be paid twice your rate. I treat my staff very well. I rarely get sick, but the boys come down with rashes and flus and things, and my wife...is dead."

"I don't work for you, sir," Dr. Gray said. "I work for the town of Utopia."

Lucien twitched slightly. "Town! There is no town. You work for me." And then Lucien Wunderfahrt's eyes became very still. "There's something boyish about you, doctor. You hardly seem a man."

Dr. Gray rubbed her chin where her beard had once been. She stood up taller. "I'm 32. It's my family. We're all young-looking. We eat beets," she muttered.

Still, the eyes kept a hawk-like fix on the doctor's face. "I see. No matter. You will be my personal physician. I am strong as bricks, but the secret to strength is to plan for times of weakness."

"Why are you really here if you are healthy?"

Again, Lucien Wunderfahrt took his time appraising the doctor with his eyes. "Just a friendly visit. I will send for you very soon." He got up, tipped his hat, and walked slowly to the door. "Get some paintings for this room." He chuckled jovially as he opened the door and exited.

Poor Montgomery rushed in when Wunderfahrt had gone. "What did he say to you?"

Dr. Gray continued unpacking her bag. "Sizing me up, I think."

Poor Montgomery scowled. "The cowboys that come into the Lilly say he's planning something big to scare us off for good."

"Then we've got to fight back," the doctor said, surprised at herself.

There was no glamour to everyday life. Christian Joseph asked Doctor Gray if he could stay with Olga Red Bootstragen and after some checking around town with people that knew the teacher well, and after a visit to the schoolhouse and the small home just down the street to meet Miss Bootstragen, the doctor consented.

He had his own room. Olga cooked and gave Christian daily chores. It was much like back in Ohio with his real parents, only Olga encouraged his writing. Olga was always in varying states of costume. Sometimes he only wore the red wig, stray ringlets hanging to his shoulders and white undershirt. Sometimes he wore a housecoat and in every remaining aspect dressed as a man. Only in public did he dress completely as a woman.

Without the wig and the women's clothing, Olga was a rather handsome thick-limbed man named Karl Frucschtemberg.

To Christian Joseph, oddly enough, Olga was both a mother and a father figure, providing a roof and three square meals a day, but most importantly, encouragement to pursue his passion – writing. Even better, Olga was a teacher, well-read, educated at Harvard, and Christian received the kind of English tutoring which, in addition to his regular studies, perfectly fitted to his aspiration to write fiction.

He attended school. There were twelve other children of varying ages and backgrounds, and they were much like the children he had known in Ohio. Some were from the Bear Mine, one from the Blacksmith Salon, and most of the rest from farms.

As much as he had escaped his family and their religious restraints, he had also lost his hero. Where was Andrew? Was he dead? What adventures had he had since they had parted back in St. Joseph? Without Andrew and his mountainous cohort, Goiter, Christian's penny novels were only cardboard substitutes.

Every day after school he passed Babe's Mercantile and Medicine Shop where he stopped to say hello to Dr. Gray and find out if there had been any sign or word from Andrew. Every day the answer was no. Back at his new home he had his homework and he had his chores.

And late at night, he would read his penny novels. He had sent away for more titles as he had read everything he had brought with him twice. Olga worked in the garden behind their house where he grew everything they ate and raised chickens. Olga was also a carpenter and made furniture.

Sometimes in the evenings after dinner, Olga would tell Christian of his lost brother and Christian got the idea to write a story called, "The Curse of the Mail Carrier," about a ghost that brought mail from the beyond. He didn't dare tell Olga of this story.

But he told him of his other writing, and he let him read what he had written from select works.

Olga became his biggest fan.

But the thrill was gone. The Adventure Spot at the railway station in Ohio was gone. He had actually boarded a train like all the people he watched and fantasized about, and he had made the journey, and there were moments of adrenaline, and Andrew had embodied the appetite Christian sought, but it was all gone.

Utopia might be a utopia, but not for the boy. It was just another place of chores and adults and repetition. He thought of all this as he hoed a row in Olga's garden. He dragged the hoe forcefully along the soil, down deep so the progress was slow. The sods became his dreams, and they were dry and dead. There was nothing in life that was like his books.

"You look like a lost orphan," Olga said.

Christian jumped a little. Had Olga been watching him all of this time?

Olga showed him a Kansas newspaper with a story about Andrew on the front page. Christian snatched it from him and devoured every word. "Kansas City Killer Found Shot Dead After Stage Coach Robbery" was the headline. Christian read: "A desperado wearing a tattered blue coat was described by the robbery victims..." It was true. Andrew was alive, and he had continued west. Even better, Andrew had killed in cold blood the worst outlaw in all the territory! There was a drawing of Andrew that did not do him justice. The caption beneath read: "Bold Bullet." Bold Bullet! The story described him traveling with a half-wit whose appearance scared children. Goiter!

"You can keep that paper, child," Olga said.

Christian Joseph thanked him. The afternoon began to shimmer. He vowed he would ask everyone he could find if they knew where Bold Bullet was or if they had heard of where he might be. He would find his hero. And he would write all about him!

The next day after school he showed the newspaper story to Dr. Gray.

"I saw that story," the doctor said. She was cleaning up after an attempt to clip an infected toenail from one of the Hairy Bears. Apparently there had been quite a struggle on the examining table.

"That means Andrew'll be arriving soon," Christian exclaimed. "He was coming here to work, wasn't he?"

"Yes," Dr. Gray said. "I expect we'll see him soon enough. You should forget about Andrew, child. He's turned bad. You keep at your studies and your writing."

Something shifted in the boy's face. He could see that, like himself, the doctor was no longer excited by the west. She had settled into a working routine. "You act like you're sad."

Dr. Gray stopped her wiping of the table with her cleaning rag. "Do I?"

"Yes'm. You kept tellin' me how different things would be out here, and you don't seem different at all, just busy. Babe says you never leave your room except to go to your office."

"You run along home, boy," Dr. Gray said. "It's none of your business what I do."

The boy's eyes widened, made anxious by the harsh and impatient tone in the doctor's voice. Without answering he hurried out the door.

Was the boy right? Doctor Gray wondered. *Am I sad? It's true; I haven't left my office or my room. Nothing about me has changed. I've been busy with my work. Every day has been solid with patients. Utopia is filled with women like me. Why haven't I announced myself to them?*

The doctor drank very seldom, but that night she asked to purchase a bottle of scotch from Babe. She took it up to her room and poured herself a double.

Fifteen minutes passed before there was a knock on the door.

"Garrison is in bed. Thought I'd join you for a nightcap." The hall gas lamp cast soft light across Babe's face.

They sat together in the two comfy chairs near the doorway.

"Kind of a recluse, eh?" Babe took a second swig.

"Been swamped."

"Why don't you stop wearing those men's clothes and that hat? Let your hair grow out a bit."

The doctor finished her first drink and poured herself a second. The buzz was strong. She'd forgotten how much relief it could bring. "I've been dressing this way for fourteen years, my entire adult life. I don't know how I'll feel if I try to change. I got rid of the beard, but this is who I am."

"Then why don't you go meet some of the women in Utopia? Let them think whatever they want. Be the real you. People understand that."

The doctor watched Babe for a moment. She took another sip. "I thought when I got to Utopia the world would feel different. I find that it doesn't."

"It's the same world and the same air. People do the same things that everyone else does out here. They work. They struggle. They live on farms. You just haven't let yourself uncoil. You've played your act so long you don't know what's beneath it."

The doctor loosened her tie, and then pulled it out from beneath her collar and tossed it recklessly on her bed. "There! How's that?"

Babe chuckled and poured herself a second scotch. "That's a start. There's a dance this Saturday. You should go. Dress however you want."

"Are you going?"

Babe blushed. "Probably, but I know everyone in town already. I've learned I'm a single gal by nature. But I like to dance. Garrison usually escorts me out."

"What about the Wunderfahrt men? Isn't a dance the perfect target for them?"

"Could be. But we can't let them intimidate us."

The doctor felt a chill. She didn't want to get too attached to the company of Babe. It dawned on her then, that she didn't want to get too attached to the company of anybody. Not even Christian Joseph or Andrew. She had been like that back in New York. She'd work long hours at the hospital and go home alone. The few women she met thought she was a man. Women, who, when they were told her secret did not turn away, and in fact, became more interested in her. She wondered if "letting go" was really what she wanted.

"Okay. I'll go to the dance."

"Who are those men on horses?" Christian Joseph asked Olga. They worked behind the house in the garden, picking tomatoes. It was Saturday morning, and the air hinted at autumn's approach.

Olga stood up and shaded his eyes. He was wearing a vanilla and cherries sundress with a floppy straw hat. Across the gulley sat five men on horseback. The men began to whistle and catcall. "Go inside, Christian," Olga said.

"Tell me who they are."

"They are cowboys from the Wunderfahrt Ranch. Go inside!"

But Christian Joseph refused. The men had driven their horses down the steep far side of the gulley, and the first man was emerging from the lip closest to them. He waved his hat, kicked his horse and galloped toward the garden.

Olga grabbed Christian with unexpected strength and lifted him up onto the back porch. Olga leapt up behind him and ran inside the house to get his rifle.

The five men on horseback trampled the garden and fired their revolvers into the air, each shot fracturing the silence with a crack.

Christian Joseph's eyes widened. "Andrew!" he cried. "Andrew! It's me, Christian Joseph!"

Andrew's eyes met the boy's, but it wasn't clear if he had heard his name called. Instead he fired his gun at a large clay pot sitting on the porch railing. The pot exploded into shards.

"Andrew!"

Olga emerged with his rifle, cocked it and fired over the cowboys' heads. They whooped and cheered and kicked their horses and galloped away back down into the gulley and up the other side.

"My garden!" cried Olga. All around them lay squashed ripe tomatoes and broken vines.

Holding onto the porch post with one hand, Christian Joseph felt tears form as he watched the cowboys thunder off toward the distant southern valley.

Saturday night as the gaslamp flickered, alone in his room, Christian Joseph wrote a list of things he had admired about Andrew.

1) Rescued him from his family.

2) Stole his father's rings.

3) Fought a gang of toughs on the waterfront.

4) Robbed a stagecoach.

5) Killed the most notorious desperado in Kansas.

6) Was not afraid to be exactly who he was.

He stared at his list for what seemed a very long time. The destruction of the garden in such a cowardly fashion just didn't fit. There was nothing brave about that. And surely Andrew would have recognized Christian Joseph. Andrew knew the boy was on his way to Utopia. Or did he forget? Did he really not care?

"I brought you some pie." Olga's voice from out in the hallway.

Christian told Olga to come in.

"Fresh out of the oven!" Olga exclaimed, and he waved the plate heaped with an oversized slice of cherry pie oozing with cherries.

Normally, Christian Joseph would be hypnotized into an eating stupor over such a sugary offering, but even his favorite pie could not rouse him.

"Depression is a terrible thing," Olga said, setting the pie plate on Christian's desk. He sat next to him on the bed and ran his hand over Christian's hair. Christian shrugged away from him. "I come from a long line of depressed people. My mother would cry her eyes out if she thought someone else might be happier than she was. She always thought she was missing out on something. She was a showgirl in

Raleigh, West Virginia. One of three. Raleigh wasn't known for its shows…"

"I'm okay," Christian said.

"No, you're not. You came all the way out here because you had a hero and now you find he's just a man. None of us are heroes. Now, help me with my party dress. We're going to that dance tonight, and you're going to be my escort."

"I don't want to go."

"Sure you do! You'll meet the other children from the valley. You might get some ideas for a new story. If we had our own newspaper you could report on what went on –"

"You don't have a newspaper? What about this?" Christian pointed to the story of Andrew in the paper he had been given.

"Heavens, no. That's from Kansas City. Hey, why don't you start a newspaper for Utopia?"

Christian Joseph suddenly inhaled a waft of cherry pie. "I'm only thirteen. I don't have a printing press. I don't know anyone."

"Is that all? If everyone went around like you do with excuses there would be no United States of America!"

"It's ridiculous. I can't start a newspaper." The boy grabbed the plate of pie and took a forkful in.

"The boys at the Screaming Lilly have a little press. They use it to make their flyers. You could talk to one of them."

It was funny, thought Christian Joseph, how one minute you could be ready to end it all and the next you could be sitting down to a feast of opportunity. All you had to do was be patient and stay alive.

"Really, Olga? Do you think I could?"

"Sure! Start small. Just one sheet at first."

"Why aren't any adults doing it?"

"Why, because we're not an official town and most people here are out on their farms and ranches or in the mines. I don't know why I didn't think of it before."

"Would you help me?" the boy asked.

"Sure I would!" Olga mussed his hair and got up. "Now let's get me presentable for the dance."

Imagine, thought Christian Joseph, as he straightened his glasses and followed Olga out into the hallway. Back in Ohio, he hadn't been allowed to go to dances or read newspapers. Dances and newspapers were the work of Mephistopheles, his parents had taught him.

As Olga held a huge scarlet party gown up in the light for inspection, Christian wondered if a newspaper was really the right thing. It certainly lacked the thrill of his dime novels. He sank deep into thought as he helped Olga search for his dancing shoes.

12. The September Shimmy

The September Shimmy was held at the Utopia Church located next to the school at the opposite end of Flume Street. Reverend Sausalito ran the church and the monthly dances had become favorites with the residents of Utopia: The August Osterich, The July Jumper, The June Jabberwalk, The May Make You Dizzy, etcetera.

Andrew found all of this out in the cowboy bunkhouse from Bastard Ass that evening. Many of the Wunderfahrt hands went to the dances and described them as "spectacles the likes of which were unheard of anywhere else," and Andrew wanted to see it.

"Don't like dances." Goiter lay prone on his top bunk.

"They won't make fun of you at this dance, Goiter," Andrew said.

"What makes you think I would be made fun of?"

"I just figured. It's a running theme with you."

Goiter snorted with derision. "It is true the kids would imitate me in Prussia. And I was the last to be asked to dance at Sing Sing."

"Suit yourself."

Goiter propped himself up on one elbow. "Aren't we supposed to be terrorizing the townspeople tonight?"

"Can't pass up a dance," Andrew said.

"Then go alone."

Goiter was tired. His constant anxiety had developed into paranoia that drained his every breath of energy. Everything had spiraled out of his control. People mistook him for a fool, but the truth was, once he got a grip on a situation, he was just as capable as any man. The thought brought him comfort. So did the bunk.

"They're lookin' for ya, you know." A voice from a bunk down below.

The voice sounded familiar. Goiter sat up with a bolt and peered over the side at the bunk beneath him and to the right. A man with a round face and shabby clothes sat up, and light from a candle near the door illuminated the weathered skin of his face.

Goiter gasped. "Charles."

"Was that really the fop you came in here with? The dandy boy with the cigarette holders?"

"Yeah."

"Hmm," Charles said.

"No, I took this job. I mean..."

Charles gave a tight laugh. "I thought you finally found out the truth, and you volunteered to kill that pansy, and here I find you two fast friends."

"What truth?"

"Carter hated your brother, but he didn't kill your brother," Charles said.

The mention of Carter from long ago and Goiter's family tragedy came as a surprise. Goiter swallowed once. "Andrew was there. He saw it happen."

"That's what he told you?" Charles said. "He didn't tell you that he pounded your brother and your brother hit his head when he fell? Sure, he saw it happen because he killed your brother in that fight at the Five Points."

Goiter felt the bunk and the earth below him disintegrate. "How do you know this?"

"My woman lived at the alley. I saw it from the window. Carter was dead drunk that day."

Goiter took a deep breath. "Andrew would have told me."

"He probably brought you out here to get rid of you."

"I don't believe it," said Goiter. "Why didn't he just leave me in New York and get away on his own somewhere?"

"Don't know. Figured you'd come after him, I guess. This way, he could bump you off and make it look like an accident. Who knows? The boys from the gang here aren't gonna let him get away with it, though. We're on your side, Goiter!"

That was odd, thought Goiter. They had never been on his side before.

And then the worrying began. This new friend might not be a friend at all. It had all been a fantasy of a friendship Goiter yearned for. Here he was stranded on the far side of the world without any ally he could trust. Nobody was ever to be trusted. He was just being used the whole time. Of course, he had always known that deep down but still his desire for a friend and to be free of New York had blinded him to the obvious. Andrew was a liar, and he had killed Goiter's brother!

The craving that had lain dormant for four months began to crawl, the aching desire to kill. This time there was a reason and an excuse to go through with it. No one would question his motives.

But I don't want to go back to prison, he thought to himself. *I must make sure I don't go back to prison.*

Goiter began to seethe inside. He hadn't done much seething before. His impulse was to go find Andrew that very instant and strangle him while everyone watched. That kind of thinking, however, had gotten him into trouble in the past. He had come too far to throw everything away. His revenge would be clever. *For once,* Goiter thought. *I will be clever!*

A bell rang from somewhere outside. Goiter became aware that Charles had been observing his reaction as Charles got to his feet and hunted about for his boots. "Ready for your first hell-ride?"

"Hell-ride?"

"Oh, that's what the boys call our little expeditions to Utopia. We raise hell."

Goiter frowned, raised himself off his bunk, and hopped down to the floor. He had been hoping for a leisurely evening, some time to rest and reflect. "Let's do it!"

On a painted banner hanging above the Utopia Church entrance could be read in huge blue letters: "The September Shimmy!"

Andrew's only companion was his stolen horse, Buchanan, whom he had named after the bachelor president. They stood off in the shadows across the street between the Blacksmith Salon and a small stable. The sun went down earlier each day as the summer waned. Nothing Andrew did made him feel comfortable. Riding, standing, sitting, smoking. Nothing calmed him. The thought of threatening people with his gun brought him no glee. The thought of actually going inside and being part of the dance party also brought him no anticipation. What would he find? More of what he left behind in New York. Stilted shallow pomposity. Misguided arrogance. Uh uh. No siree, brother. He wasn't going to be part of more of the same.

People began gathering inside. A small band sat near the church organ, three hairy white men, one with a banjo and two with fiddles. Several church people tied green ribbons to the picket fence posts. A wagon pulled up and two women, one white and one Black, unloaded what looked to be all manner of cakes and food.

None of the people Andrew observed looked like the men at the parties he attended back in New York. But they didn't look like regular homesteaders either. Some of the men looked strong and rugged, others were more like the city men Andrew was used to, but even they walked with a certain swagger that showed they were unconcerned with whoever might be watching. Even more astounding, they seemed used to not having anyone watching them!

Andrew tied Buchanan to the fence by the stable, determined to go inside the church and see what the losers were really like.

He had sauntered to the front gate of the little churchyard when coming down the walk from the center of town, he saw a very tall woman wearing a scarlet flounced skirt and a heavily trimmed pink bonnet, and a boy that looked like Christian Joseph St. Martin. When the boy saw him, he stopped still.

"What's the matter?" the woman asked the boy. She followed his gaze and laid eyes on Andrew. "Just ignore him," she said. She tried to pull him along, but he remained rooted to the spot, keeping a steady lock on Andrew.

She dropped his hand and looked about to lecture him, when he marched quickly and resolutely toward Andrew. He pressed his lips tightly together and looked Andrew up and down.

"We made it!" Andrew said, to break the ice. "Here now, I didn't know that was you this afternoon. We meant no harm. How is the doctor?"

"You're nothing like the people in my books."

Andrew had never particularly liked children, but this boy's words winded him. "Nobody is like the people in your books, boy," Andrew said.

"You rescued me from my family in Ohio. I thought you were something more."

"Look, I took you with me because I felt sorry for you," Andrew said.

"Well, don't!" Christian Joseph exclaimed. "You left me with the doctor."

Andrew put his hands on his hips. Several groups of men, some of them handsome, passed them on the walk on their way to the church gate. "And what did you think I would be? Your new father?"

Muscles in Christian Joseph's face tightened. "I wouldn't want you to be my father after you and your friends trampled Olga's garden. You don't care anything about other people. That's plain."

The hate in the boy's eyes flickered.

Andrew avoided looking at the boy as he let them pass. He stood there alone feeling a faint chill for several moments as more of the residents of Utopia, dressed in their finery, approached for their evening of fun.

He entered Utopia Church still surprised at how much the boy's words bothered him. The floor had been cleared for dancing, and a huge white wooden cross hung suspended over the podium dominating the room. The band had set up just below the minister's station and played a lively rendition of a song Andrew had not heard. The banjo player sang the lyrics. His voice plaintive but assured.

"What is that song?" Andrew asked a strapping homesteader.

"The Rest of the West," the man answered, and then gave Andrew a curious look.

The lyrics fascinated him as the violin and banjo played:

Meet me, my love

beneath the skies

and shed your city

and its lies

for here we join and here we dance

and here is found

our true romance

People clapped, and two women Andrew recognized from the corner Chinese laundry danced together. One wore cowboy garb and yet her face retained a beauty that no society woman back in New York could ever claim. The other dancer was by all accounts a typical western townswoman, with turquoise ribbons in her hair.

"You're new in the valley?" Andrew's tall acquaintance asked.

Andrew nodded in agreement. Nowhere did he see the pasty feigned arrogance of the parties he had known in New York.

"You want to dance with me?" the man asked.

Andrew had only come to observe and had expected to leave quickly with his pre-formed judgments confirmed. He turned to look at the cowboy next to him for the first time. The man's eyes were almond brown and contained no trace of insecurity. He was ruggedly handsome, face freshly shaved, hair slicked back. "I mean," he said. "I just love to dance. Get a little whiskey in me, and I can't stop."

A terrible sadness pulled at Andrew from inside and sank from his eyebrows to his stomach. "No, thanks."

"Oh well, then. Nice to meet ya!" The cowboy gave Andrew another curious look and then turned and asked the man on his other side for a dance. They took the dance floor, and his suitor hooked his thumbs through his belt loops and held his hat with his right hand as he commenced a lively jig. His partner clapped his hands, and Andrew observed nothing less than two full-blooded men enjoying themselves.

From different parts of the increasingly populated room, he noticed men looking at him. Not society intellectuals sending him coded signals, and not drunken dockworkers in backrooms of Hell's Kitchen sending him sneers filled with mixed messages. Here, the men were unabashedly interested and curious.

A group of children gathered in the corner by the food table where they had been served small cakes. Christian Joseph stood among them. The boy spotted Andrew and scowled at him across the full length of the room.

Andrew's pride at not fitting in had no place in this room, and the realization at once terrorized him. The men were a cut far above the limited souls back east. How was this possible?

He needed opium. He needed booze.

Christian Joseph became so angry he even refused Olga's famous inside-out cake. As the room grew more crowded his anger changed to curiosity. All of the couples were men with men and women with women, although he couldn't always be sure. They walked arm in arm whispering into each other's ears, or they danced and held hands. Several stole kisses from each other. During his travels west he had heard Andrew describe his true nature, but the details had been vague. Now, here it was in vivid real life!

His pious family had raised him to believe that this type of behavior was caused by demons who inhabited the weak and who could squirt themselves out of sinners' bodies and infect the righteous like the stomach flu. Two boys holding hands was the equivalent of cannibalism.

Like so many of the teachings of his minister father and family, Christian Joseph disregarded what he had been told. He knew that his father gambled and that his mother flirted with the chimney sweep and that his older sister threw rocks at the flowers in the yard. These practices were all deeply held family secrets that only his investigative journalism had brought to light. Only he knew. And it was enough to distance him from anything extolled by religious men.

Still, the actual site of people of the same sex or of questionable affinities expressing affection without shame was not something he had seen before. And there stood Andrew looking lost.

Dr. Gray remained as far off in the corner in the back as possible while Babe helped with the food tables across the room. The Doctor wore her freshly pressed brown pants, black laced-up boots, and a plain white dress shirt tied loosely with a black silk cravat. Over the shirt she wore a brown vest. Her hat was gone and her face was clean of all traces of the phony beard. She had allowed her hair to begin growing out, but it was still cut short like a man.

With horror, Dr. Gray noticed Babe motioning to her to come over to the food tables directly across the room. The doctor indicated a vehement "no." Babe made an exasperated face and repeated her hand gesture to come over to the table.

Several of Dr. Gray's patients were helping with the food display. The beautiful and razor-direct Pooja Aswani laid a dish of cocoanut curry on a large cloth napkin. Her wife, as she called her, was an escaped servant from Florida known as Sky. They both stood by the punch bowl, sipping from crystal glasses and surveying the room.

No one seemed to recognize the doctor. Feeling tension in her jaw and a disturbing urge to run out the door into the street, the doctor put out her right foot and stepped forward.

She had practiced so long how to walk like a man and not be sus-pected of fraud, hiding behind a beard, she felt entirely self-conscious, completely exposed and foolish. Her feet were the size of snowshoes. Her hands were big as water bags. She was neither sex.

This is ludicrous, she thought to herself, half way across the still mostly empty dance floor. She took on a functional stride, purely meant to get her where she was going. This would take some getting used to. She told herself to relax. For the first time, rather than fit in, she could just be herself comfortable in clothes she wanted to wear.

This could be fun, Dr. Gray thought, although she felt like she was twelve years old all over again.

"You did good," Babe said when Dr. Gray arrived at the table of jams and preserves near the fried chicken. "You looked like you were marching to the gallows but you did it! I'm proud of ya!"

Dr. Gray allowed herself to relax and help Babe with putting food out on the tables. Pooja and Sky shrieked with happy surprise when Babe told them who she was. She no longer had to worry about being found out. There would be no awkward moments later after having met someone and going somewhere private and telling the shocked woman she had chosen that she was not in fact, a man, but a woman wearing a phony beard.

Too many times she had simply foregone the admission and all the attendant humiliation and anxiety, and simply let the unsuspecting date go on thinking she was Dr. Troy Reed. Just think, thought the doctor now, no more kissing women through that wretched phony beard. No more explaining that the reason she was so slight of build and slender of hand was because of a childhood illness resulting in reduced blood platelets.

The icing on the cake, she thought, is that I get to remain being a doctor and doing all the things I want to do. There are no restrictions.

I can walk into a saloon without an escort. I can walk down the street alone and not be thought of as a whore. I can live like a man without pretending to be one!

She waved at Ricardo and his date, Benito, the bakers she had treated for bee stings a week before. Dr. Gray began to hum. She served herself chicken fried steak with a biscuit and gravy.

Eight o'clock came and there were close to ninety people gathered in the church dance hall. Paper lanterns glowed red and white and gold. The dancing included everyone now, even those alone or in groups on the sidelines. The children danced in their own circles.

Christian Joseph had lost sight of Andrew. He had forgotten himself in the excitement of the evening, the abundance of food and sweets, and the new friends from school that he was sharing stories with. The dance was much more fun than anything he had known in Ohio.

Andrew headed for the door. The dance hall was too brightly lit and the people too exposed. The cowboy grabbed his shoulder from behind. "What's the hurry, good-lookin? You just got here."

"Can't stay."

"Why not? You look like you need it."

"What's that supposed to mean?"

"You can drop the tough crap with me, buddy," the cowboy said. "You got city-boy written all over ya. What? Did ya get hired by the Wunderfahrts to try to terrorize the poor strange citizens of Utopia? And you've convinced yourself you're working under cover comin' to this dance? You don't know how popular we are with all the tough guys. Tough? What does that mean, anyways?"

The brown-eyed cowboy had utterly dismantled him. What was worse, he had the nerve to stare Andrew down afterward, waiting, apparently for some kind of explanation of himself.

"You all think you're bettern' us," the cowboy went on. "And the truth is, you're the worse for it. Most of the ranch hands at the Big W know that. All they and probably you want is the money."

The cowboy snorted once with derision, in a knowing chuckle. "People always gotta think they're bettern' somebody else. That's how we keep track of ourselves, by comparison."

"Maybe you think you're better than me," Andrew said.

The cowboy appeared amused. "Maybe I do. Why don't we find out?" He extended his arm to Andrew and indicated the dance floor.

But Andrew didn't accept the invitation. There was no witty retort to be made. There was no dismissive remark he could think of. There was nothing. Nothing but a jangling thrilling confusion and terror.

Back in New York when he was Clay Van Torte, he knew the rules. He could be seen at public gatherings with Senator Hawkins and introduced as an "aide." In public they must act as if they were devoted to their wives. They could never touch except behind closed doors. Large parties sometimes were held for men like themselves who all played the same game and sent coded signals to each other with eye contact or with sly innuendo. No one told the truth. No one wasn't hollow inside.

He had known nothing else.

Into the night he hurried. Down the street he ran toward the gaslights surrounding the gaudily painted sign for "The Screaming Lilly Saloon."

"This way, Bold Bullet," came a whisper from the dark.

Andrew moved cautiously around the corner and into the shadows behind the saloon. Several of Wunderfahrt's men waited for him there. Muted pianoforte music tinkled from inside along with whoops and hollers from several male voices.

The Screaming Lilly stood three stories tall. In the back grew scrag-gily apple trees barren this time of year, near wicker chairs and a gilt iron love seat set haphazardly in the yard. Dark windows graced each level of the building. The early hour and the dance had taken much of the Lilly's business.

Goiter stood holding a broom smelling of vodka. He glared at Andrew. His expression was one Andrew hadn't seen directed at him, cold and filled with malice. His blue cloth cap showed a gaping tear. He wore the collar on his tattered coat turned up. One of the other men struck a match and lit the broom head. Goiter tossed the flaming spear up and over the sill of an open window.

Another of Wunderfahrt's men climbed an apple tree and they watched as he lit a ball of rags and tossed the flame bomb through the open window of the top floor. The room lit up and something inside caught fire.

They handed Andrew a ball of alcohol-soaked rags tied to a stick. One of the men lit it. Andrew hesitated only a moment and chose to ignore a faint voice in his head. He grit his teeth and tossed the fireball into a second floor window. What did he care about a ratty bar two thousand miles from New York? If they had been in Manhattan he would have gladly set fire to the pseudo intellectual fetes. They were gatherings of lies and they only created heartbreak and men like the Senator.

Time was limited now. The rest of the men quickly lit their projec-tiles and flung them at all of the open windows. Explosions of light and flames popped and danced inside two more rooms.

They ran for their horses.

"Fire!" they heard shouted behind them. A larger explosion burst from another one of the rooms. "Fire! The Screaming Lilly is on fire!"

Andrew ran down the street to where Buchanan was tied across from the dance and the church. Burning smoke filled the air. The running and rush of energy it gave him cleared his mind of doubt.

He heard hooves pounding the hard dirt of the street and swung around to see three horsemen gallop into the blackness at the edge of town. Wunderfahrt's men, he muttered to himself feeling a hard tension in his forehead.

People began to dash out of the dance hall. Several men and women in pants ran past him to horses. "Fire! They set fire to the Lilly!"

Andrew watched his cowboy clomp out in his boots onto the wooden walkway in front of Utopia Church. He pushed his hat onto his head and turned to face the north end of the street to get a look at the burning saloon. His eyes passed over Andrew and it was clear he recognized him. Andrew saw him glare with the recognition and then dash off toward the Screaming Lilly Saloon.

More ranch hands on horseback galloped down the road. They shot pistols in the air while their horses reared and kicked their legs. Over the whinnying of the horses, the men catcalled and roared with laughter and whoops of glee. They fired more shots and then galloped away while several clusters of townspeople gathered and jeered.

The tongues of golden flame leapt in and out from the upper windows of the Screaming Lilly. Men and women with buckets dipped water from the horse troughs while someone drove a wagon with barrels in the back to the saloon entrance. People ran in all directions.

Glancing back at the church he saw a boy standing alone, glowering at him. It was Christian Joseph St. Martin. Sizing him up, no doubt, as he always did, and each time lowering his opinion of Andrew, like so many others in Andrew's life had done before.

"Him! He did it! I saw him do it!" Christian Joseph shouted pointing his index finger directly at Andrew.

His boots and body didn't belong to him. His tattered blue jacket felt wrong. The entire scene was a broken snow globe and he a small wooden figure that had fallen out.

Disoriented and ashamed, he hurried toward his horse and left the boy behind.

13. What Dreams Can Burn?

The Screaming Lilly Saloon lit the sky with fire.

Bailey, the Swedish owner, late forties, gray whiskers, and a full head of obviously imitation thick blond hair, bent way over and gasped for air as smoke billowed from the entrance to his saloon.

Shouts and cries for more water buckets by the townspeople came from inside the two-story wood frame bordello. All sorts of men in various states of undress rushed about visible intermittently through the dark fumes.

Candleman, the "sailor" rushed shirtless up to Bailey from the boardwalk. He was a sailor but he had never been to sea.

"Bailey! I've got you!" He held his boss with his strong bare arms as dark lanterns of smoke floated eerily down the main street of Utopia.

Bailey's eyes grew red around the rims and dirty tears smeared the soot on his cheeks. He patted the thick fingers of the sailor, and stood to his full height. He shook both fists across the valley at the Wunderfahrt Ranch. "I won't lose everything I've worked my whole life for!"

he shouted, his toupee askew. The heat had apparently loosened the spirit gum.

"They're gonna wanna buy you out," the sailor shouted into Bailey's ear. "The Wunderfahrts will try to buy you out like they bought out the Water Mill women."

Bailey gripped the huge bicep of the sailor, and let the whore assist him to the boardwalk and back to help with quenching the fire. "I'll ride that Gretchen Wunderfahrt around like a circus pony before I let that happen!"

The sailor grunted in unsure agreement.

"And I'll fire bullets at her old father's feet and make him dance for his dinner!"

The sailor reached for a bucket full of water that one of the younger men handed him. As he did so, he stole a glance at the lights of the Wunderfahrt Ranch House far across the valley.

Black shadows crawled slowly over Utopia.

Distant shouts and long fingers of smoke floated across the valley, up the hill, and to the window of the parlor of the ranch house that belonged to Lucien Wunderfahrt. Gretchen watched from behind the beveled glass as the smoke rose in a small black coil against the gray-green of the Wyoming prairie.

She crept away from the window. "Why does that old man hate me?" she grumbled to herself. "I made this fire for him. Madchen is dead! Dead ten years!"

She folded her arms and glared bitterly at the oil portrait of Madchen hanging above the hearth. An admittedly beautiful young woman with light blond hair "the color of the sunshine in spring," her father announced repeatedly. Madchen had gone to college. Madchen made her own ceramics. Madchen could speak Italian.

Gretchen felt her hands clench into fists.

Next to Madchen's portrait hung that of Gretchen. As much as she had tried, Gretchen's attempt at a regal and delicate smile had resulted in something a taxidermist might have molded on the lips of a dead owl. Even her oil portrait was inferior to the damn Madchen!

Lucien Wunderfahrt lit his pipe and observed his daughter through narrowed eyes. His head ached. What was she babbling about now?

Gretchen's figure stood artfully camouflaged by gray puffs of fabric in her angular Canter's dress. Her long face and oval eyes always appeared anxious and tired. Shapeless brown hair swirled clumsily away from her face and drooped in a bunch tied in back. "You wanted that Devil's House burned, Father! I made it happen for you!"

Lucien Wunderfahrt exhaled blue haze.

"Still thinking about Madchen's memorial?" Gretchen demanded bitterly. "What has she done for you lately? I graduate from college and you are bored. I nursed you back to health after your horse kicked you in the face. I rebuilt the barn after the Big Storm of '53. I hired your nurse and then had her arrested. All for you! You should love me! Madchen is dead!"

Lucien Wunderfahrt was sixty-eight. He had long white bushy sideburns and a shiny bald scalp. He wore wooden dentures from Italy that shifted and fell out frequently, and caused him to curse the Lord. Yet, he had lightning reflexes with his gun, and he could still trot down a dirt road very fast.

"I do smell the inferno." Lucien bit into an imported cracker. "Son bitch teeth! That valley is mine, by rights, and the hills and the river. Manifest Destiny and Wunderfahrt's Law!" Lucien Wunderfahrt shouted, cracker spraying from his mouth.

The old man leaned far in across the silver cutlery on the table. His white tie brushed the chicken gravy on his plate. The wrinkles around his eyes and on his cheeks collected into bunches. "This fire and the last one are not enough. We must terrify those people. You and your sister. You all must help."

"Madchen is dead."

Lucien leaned back in his velvet red chair. "Yes, I knew that. Her spirit permeates this house. She made this tablecloth."

"A plantation in Virginia, actually, Father. She sent them a design, that's all!"

"Dammit, child!" Lucien slammed his fist onto the tabletop. "Ouch. Jesus! My neck." He adjusted his teeth.

Gretchen observed the old man as a sheepherder might observe a particularly difficult sheep to sheer. Yet again, she vowed he would give her the credit she deserved.

The smoke still lingered in Bailey's lungs when he heard the child cry out and point at a man leading his horse toward them down the road. Bailey clutched at his throat, coughed deep and hard, and fought to stand up tall.

"That's one of the Wunderfahrt men," he gasped when the sailor tried to hold him back. Bailey shrugged off the sailor's grasp and reached for the pistol he kept pocketed under his bar apron.

"That's Bold Bullet," the sailor warned him. "He shot the Kansas City Killer."

"Maybe so." Bailey stood up full.

"I don't want no trouble with you," Andrew called out when Bailey faced him from twenty yards. "I'll be on my way."

"The hell you will." Bailey drew his gun and cocked the hammer.

Andrew did the same. "Go tend your bar, barkeep."

"You mean my ashes?" Bailey took a half step forward and aimed his pistol at Andrew's face.

Andrew shot him in the chest.

Shouts and snaps from the burning saloon muted the crack of the gunshot, but the children in front of the dancehall heard it and they covered their ears in terror.

The sailor ran toward Bailey but not fast enough to catch him before his face hit the dirt.

Andrew's breathing picked up. He pressed his lips hard together to hold back what felt like an avalanche of stress. He trembled with the familiar adrenaline rush, the heightened senses, the feeling of purpose, and he heard the metal click of another gun near the church gate, behind the hedgerow. He turned and fired in one motion and a moment after the blast tore Andrew's ears a man fell over, dead, on the plank walkway to the sound of screaming children.

Around him came the shouts from the women and the sailor whore. In the distance he could see men dropping buckets and rushing out to find out the cause of the commotion. Andrew mounted his horse, jerked its head east, and lit off toward the east valley and the safety of the Wunderfarht Ranch.

14. In League With The Devil

Poor Montgomery paced back and forth. He wore no shirt beneath his blue suspenders, and no shoes or socks. He was 6'3 and lanky. "No. No. I'm not asking him to send me a box of confections. The Screaming Lilly Saloon burned to the ground last night! Andrew's daddy is a lawyer. A mean ol' lawyer and he can help us fight those Wunderfahrts!"

Akers was an officer in the cavalry. He was used to orders, but not coming from his favorite rent boy. Well, maybe sometimes, but only orders taken in bed during jolly frolics. The cabin they had rented was just out of town. The room was cold and bare. Akers yearned for the warmth that Poor Montgomery's affection could provide. If they could just hurry up and finish this damned letter...

Poor Montgomery scratched the sparse hair on the center of his chest. "All my clothes were burned! All I got left are these britches. Where are us boys going to work now? I saw the one they call Goiter start the fire. He's a sickun! And poor Bailey? What're we gonna do without Bailey and his bar? Huh? I was startin' to make somethin' of myself!"

"I can't write that fast, Monty!"

Poor Montgomery blinked his tired eyes and came over to the sorry wooden table. He bent down so close to Akers that Akers could feel the rent boy's whiskers brush his own face. "Don't write any of that last stuff down! I was thinkin'!"

Akers slammed his pen down on the paper in an angry splotch of ink. He placed his hands defiantly on his large love handles. "How am I supposed to know when you are thinkin' and when you are dictatin'? I ain't no mind reader. I ain't no crystal ball watcher. I only got an hour and you're wastin' it."

Poor Montgomery stood up full and glared down at Akers as if Akers were an enormous bedbug found crawling in fresh linens. "You listen here, Petrie Akers. If we don't do something about those evil Wunderfahrts there won't be any more hours with me or anyone like me, you understand? You went to school but I got the smarts seems like. There won't be any more Screamin' Lilly Saloon, and you'll go home every night to your wife and she'll just lie there waitin' for you to get it over with and that'll be your romancin'. O what heaven that will be!"

Akers turned a pale ash color.

Poor Montgomery cleared his throat and went back to the window where he could see the remaining buildings of downtown Utopia on the horizon. "Read that letter back to me now, real nice. We'll post it to old Mr. Van Torte and I'll let you ride behind me on my horse when we ride back into town."

Bailey's body lay on a makeshift table made from two sawhorses and plywood planks, waiting for the mortician's wagon. At least his death had been quick, Doctor Gray determined.

She exited her back room office wearing the same outfit from the night before, and stepped out into the dry air. The smell of sweet sagebrush could not remove the fear that she was responsible for the beloved bartender's death. It was she who had brought Andrew to Utopia. Her idea.

The man who had been her closest friend in New York, whom she had understood, she thought, better than anyone in the world had turned bad. He was a murderer.

She took several steps in hopes of initiating a mind-clearing walk, but she was stymied by indecision. If she had misjudged Andrew so completely, perhaps she couldn't be sure of anything else she believed.

Preposterous! She marched resolutely toward the garden and again she halted herself. She had also believed she would find herself in Utopia. At the dance, without the beard and the put-on swagger, she mostly felt disoriented. Maybe Utopia was a mistake.

The thought frightened her because she had not foreseen it. Rather than agonize any further over core personal decisions, she hurried back to her back room office and the cold corpse of the murdered bartender.

Gretchen Wunderfahrt offered Andrew a brandy.

"It's opium for me," Andrew muttered. He couldn't bring himself to look Gretchen in the eyes. The adrenaline of the night before had long since receded replaced by a cold guilt. Yes, he had shot Bailey and the other man in self-defense. What was different was those men were defending their property from attack...from the people who hired him and from himself.

"Ooh. I love opium!" Gretchen exclaimed. She wore a quail blue riding outfit and a little cap which was small for her outsized forehead. "But Daddy said he'd cut off all my hair if I ever smoked opium, so I can't do it around here." They sat in the back parlor, the parlor used for greeting clothes launderers and making illicit wagers with mid-level passing banditos, and Gretchen knew not what else. The decor was ragtag compared to the opulence of the front parlors. There was even a vulgar pet stain on the worn Elizabethan throw rug. Gretchen sucked on her sip of scotch and leaned forward conspiratorily with Andrew. "You killed the bar owner? They say you did."

"Who?"

"The boys in the bunkhouse. You killed another man, too. They're calling you Bold Bullet."

Andrew swigged his drink. "I only defended myself."

"No one is colorful like you. They're just thugs. But you..." Gretchen indicated with her hands Andrew's long and precisely combed hair, his black nails, and the black liner around his eyes. "...you come out here wearing brass buttons and blue silk. You are someone people talk about. You're just the man we've been looking for to lead my boys. To buy out the perverts in the valley."

Andrew felt his jaw tighten. "Ma'am, I am also one of those 'perverts' as you put it."

Gretchen Wunderfahrt's warm scotch buzz disappeared. She swallowed despite having already swallowed her last sip. And then she grunted once with irony. "I thought I'd found my man." She turned the rock glass around in her hand and examined it as if it had once held diamonds. Jilted again. Why even try? These men never meant what they said and when they did their sincerity evaporated away with the dawn.

The tension built in her neck as she glanced back up at Andrew. "Why are you fighting against your own people, then?"

Andrew poured himself another drink from the crystal decanter. "Another list. My people always have to be put on a list. I hate lists. I like money. I like excitement."

"So do I!" Gretchen exclaimed bitterly. She got up and walked over to the back window which opened out offering a view of the Wunderfahrt Mountains in the afternoon sun, and the cool shadowed sagebrush dotting the foothills.

"There are people like me everywhere I go," Andrew said. "Why do I need to live in a special town?"

"Those townspeople don't keep secrets, I guess," Gretchen said, a somber tone in her voice. "Secrets can be terrible things."

Andrew placed his empty drink glass on a little table with a smack. "Depends on the secret."

Gretchen turned to face her star terrorist. "I don't care if you are a pervert. There are all kinds of perverts, if you call sinning a perversion. I'll double your salary if you keep up the good work. Go into town with my father and offer those people money for all their houses. Now's the time to strike while they're still bruised from last night."

Andrew tipped his hat.

"I've got a new man arriving to help you. Charles wired back east for him and I'm told Utopia won't survive. I'm sure you won't mind."

After a moment's hesitation Andrew replied, "No."

"Wait," Gretchen said, before he could turn to go. "Even if you are a pervert, did you really mean it the other day when you said you fancied me?"

Andrew half-grinned at her. "Of course, I did," he lied.

Gretchen considered him a moment. She cocked her head slightly to the left and looked him up and down. "Get out of here, gunslinger. Maybe we'll have another drink together soon."

The valley shimmered in golds and reds. Late September had turned the leaves of the Quaking Aspen early that year. Dr. Gray struggled to appreciate the beauty. The little carriage that had been sent for her by old man Wunderfahrt smelled of new leather. The sides were open, but she could not revel in the clean air, the smell of clean white gravel, or the scrub brush along the road.

The gravel crunched beneath the carriage wheels as Dr. Gray was driven to the marble front steps of the Ranch House.

The driver seemed unsure whether to help her down or not. The doctor ran her hand awkwardly over her bare cheeks. Her man's outfit, this time sans the vest, most likely confused him. She shooed him aside. The three-story mansion stood solidly before her, a great edifice in the untrammeled country.

Far across the lane toward the west, she observed Andrew walking briskly toward the bunkhouse. He saw her, hesitated, and then approached her.

"You killed the Lilly's owner," she said when he stood before her. "I declared him dead in my office. And you shot one of the Lilly boys."

"I shot in self-defense."

"You set fire to the Lilly."

"The land belongs to old man Wunderfahrt."

"I saw you at the dance that night. Looked like you did pretty well for yourself, if you would have let the cowboy dance with you."

"You abandoned me in St. Joseph," Andrew said.

"I'd say it was the other way around."

"Why are you here?"

"Mr. Wunderfahrt needs a doctor."

"So, you're no better than me," Andrew said.

The doctor shook her head. "It's not the same thing."

"Isn't it?"

The doctor frowned. "No."

"What do you want with me?"

"Nothing anymore," the doctor said. "I had a friend once."

She hesitated a moment. When Andrew's expression didn't change, she turned and walked with a heavy heart toward the front door of the Wunderfahrt ranch house.

"Well, well." Goiter crossed his arms over his chest. Rarely did Goiter get anyone over a barrel, and he savored the moment.

"Not now, Goiter," Andrew said.

Goiter knew how taxing it could be to kill a man. Many times after murdering someone, Goiter required a nap. He almost felt empathy for the fop.

They were the only two in the bunkhouse. The others had all gone off to their various tasks around the ranch. None had gone into town, the fire and killings were enough for the time being.

Andrew tossed his hat on his bunk.

"You killed my brother," Goiter said.

There was only the slightest hesitation in the dandy's movements as he sat down and began to remove his boots.

Goiter watched intently to see if anything changed in the fop's body language. Sure enough, there was a waver to Andrew's eyes and a slight muscle movement in his cheek. Andrew shook his head once as if to clear it. "What?"

"You lied to me all along."

"No, I didn't."

Andrew's tone was the intonation someone used when scolding a dog. Goiter was tired of being treated like a dog.

For a moment, neither of the men moved.

Goiter felt the craving rise up inside of him. Andrew was a fast draw. He might shoot Goiter. Goiter did not want to be shot. If he survived he might suffer long weeks of infection and perhaps might lose a limb. He might die in the back of a hospital wagon. If he did not survive a gunshot, well, he'd be dead. Being dead terrified Goiter.

Sweat beads formed on Goiter's forehead.

"What are you going to do, Goiter? You going to murder me, is that it?" Andrew asked. "We're friends. I got you out of New York."

"I got me out of New York," Goiter said.

"You never would have left if it weren't for me."

"Tell me about my brother."

Andrew stood up. "Your brother hated men like me. He used to brag how he beat up fops and drowned them in the river. He followed me into that alley and wanted me to fight. I pushed him away and he hit his head on the steps. He died instantly. I left him there because I didn't trust anyone to believe it was an accident. I'm sorry."

Goiter felt tension around his eyes. He waited, but Andrew wouldn't say any more. He was surprised to notice that his craving to kill Andrew had been replaced by an aching loneliness. He lowered his eyes and backed away from the bunks and from Andrew, toward the open door. He gripped the doorframe, never looked up, turned, and walked out toward the horses to be far away from people.

The bunkhouse was hot, and Andrew decided to lie down, facing the door. If Goiter returned in a rage, Andrew would be ready. How tiresome it was to always be on the defensive. Things happened the way they did. There was nothing Goiter or anyone could do to change them.

The feelings from killing the two men in town weren't like those from his shooting of the Kansas City Killer. The difference was these men were residents of Utopia. They were men like Andrew.

To ease the pain he tried thinking of the cowboy at the dance. Not so much because the cowboy was attractive, which he was, but that he was someone different. The cowboy's handshake and the peace of his brown eyes mystified Andrew.

Yet it wasn't enough to erase the memory of the hate in the eyes of Christian Joseph and the feeling of not being oneself...ever. It wasn't enough to forget killing Bailey and the other man at the burning saloon. Andrew wanted to get drunk and smoke opium and disappear, but what good was that? What good was any of it?

He thought it odd when a smile formed on his lips.

"Yes?" Lucien Wunderfahrt sat in a large brown leather chair behind an oak desk trimmed in brass. His bald head contrasted with the rich leather behind him.

Dr. Gray entered the old man's library. "You sent for me?" She noticed movement through the beveled glass window and spied Andrew on his horse loaded with a full saddlebag galloping toward town.

The old rancher knitted his fingers together beneath his chin. "I know you're not a born-man. I hear tell you used to wear a beard. Maybe that disguised you better." He squinted at her. "I don't know why women aren't allowed to be doctors."

"Technically we are. But it's near impossible," Dr. Gray said. "Black women in particular."

"I lied before. I'm dyin'. The last doctor to see me told me I had the cancer, a tumor that he could feel on my right side." The rancher indicated exactly where with his right hand. "The lump has grown bigger since the doctor saw me. He had said the only hope was to have it cut out."

"Where did your doctor go? How long ago?"

"We shot him. About four months."

The doctor took a step closer. "Why did you shoot him?"

"He killed my little girl." Lucien Wunderfahrt's voice cracked on the word "little." "He gave her the wrong medicine for the consumption, and she died the next day. He poisoned her. Poor Madchen…"

"Still, that's no reason to shoot someone."

"Blast!" Lucien Wunderfahrt smacked his desk with his fist and rose instantly to his feet. "He murdered her because she refused his proposal! It was murder, and we meted out his punishment."

"I better go." Dr. Gray took several steps to the door.

"No! I will die if you don't help me."

"You are terrorizing the people in your own town. Two men died last night because of what you instigated. Let nature take its course."

"Are those the words of a woman of medicine?"

"In this instance, yes," said Dr. Gray.

"If you don't help me there are bounty hunters who could fetch a very high price for a Black doctor back in Louisiana."

Dr. Gray felt her breathing quicken. For a long time, she didn't speak a word and didn't give an answer to the bald man facing her in the shadowed pockets of the Ranch Library.

"And after that," Lucien Wunderfahrt said, "I will kill your little boy. The one you arrived in town with. His name is Christian, I believe."

15. MORTIS

There was something freeing about being totally disgusted with yourself. Goiter's mind cleared of all its endless anxious minutia. Nothing mattered. Everything was uniformly hopeless. He found himself almost reborn as he walked slowly back to the bunkhouse. Since his entire self-perception had been incorrect, he could start afresh. He could hate who he had been and start completely over hating himself more than anyone else.

A huge shadow filled the doorway, so large Goiter thought it must be an illusion. He came to a stop. "Who's there?"

"Ah yes. The sun is going down." A deep and confident voice. "Your day is coming to an end."

Goiter felt a tingle of nerves.

A short chuckle came from the dark. "Did you really think the gang would send you out west to kill the fop and let you both disappear?"

Goiter turned slightly.

"It's not too late. We can make a team."

"Team?" Weariness flooded Goiter. "I pick the wrong people to trust."

"I'm the right people." The man stepped out from the doorway. *He must be six foot five*, thought Goiter, *taller than Elroy Moot back in the Five Corners.* He had red hair and wore a long black tracker's coat. Dark stubble covered his cheeks, and his boots crunched the pebbles underfoot. *This is what a real assassin looks like*, Goiter realized, *not some dope like me.*

"You don't need me," Goiter said.

"No. But you need me. Your stagecoach victims were discovered and gave very detailed descriptions of you. And then Charles wired me in Kansas City."

"Who are you?"

Another chuckle. "Just joined the Wunderfahrt ranch hands. My name is Mortis."

Goiter spent the rest of the afternoon with Mortis. They smoked cigarettes that made Goiter cough. Mortis drank whiskey that Goiter pretended to sip. Mortis taught Goiter how to whittle a little coffin out of beechwood. All the while, Goiter racked his brain for an escape plan. The gang had associates all over the country and out west. News traveled fast by telegraph. There was no hope.

"It's really very simple," Mortis said. "You could hold his head down in a bucket of water and hit him with a hammer. I did that once to a divorce lawyer in Laredo. I didn't even get wet."

Goiter shook his head in horror like he understood.

"You could pretend to make it up to him and put your arm around his neck. I've broken three men's necks and one nun's with my bare hands. Like I said, I hate blood. It stains my shirts, and I like my shirts."

Goiter nodded again in grim affirmation.

"You'll have to do it this week, I'm afraid. I can't wait any longer than that," said Mortis.

"Or what...will happen?"

"I will kill you and kill the fop myself." The tone in Mortis's voice was bone cold. "I'll ship you back to the gang in tiny little boxes to prove the job is done. You don't want to know how."

"But if I kill him in front of witnesses how will I stay free?"

"You have your work cut out for you then, don't you? You really must do your homework. Didn't anyone ever teach you that?"

Goiter lowered his head. No one had ever taught him that. He had never had a mentor. Perhaps, he thought, that was one reason he had liked Andrew. Andrew was someone he could learn from. But Andrew was a liar, and Goiter could no longer look up to him. He was all alone again.

He stood up, spat, and trembled when Mortis stood up next to him. "I'll do it."

Mortis spat with more force. "Dandies deserve to be dead. They are inverts and animals. They are useless aberrations." And he draped his thick arm over Goiter's shoulder.

16. NOT ONE OF US

Outside the smoldering remains of the Screaming Lilly Saloon, Poor Montgomery took a healthy bite from a fried chicken leg. Smudges of soot still clung to his arms and pants from the fire the day before.

Regino, the former barback, toyed with a dollop of tapioca on his spoon. He was fifty-one and had been very handsome once. He was still good-looking, but in a "I've known a lot of pain" way. "This is a sad little picnic."

"We can thank Babe for givin' us this luncheon basket." The sailor pulled a biscuit apart and then pushed each piece into his mouth. "What are we going to do now? Farms make me allergic."

"My boy," Regino laid his spoon meticulously down on a plaid country napkin. "You don't need to change careers. You can do your kind of work anywhere with an awning or a fence. We will rebuild. Bailey started the Screaming Lilly with just a tarp and four small trees. We are survivors. We are winners. We are..." Regino bowed his head and sobbed.

"I knew it would hit him sometime." Poor Montgomery leaned forward and patted his co-worker on the back.

The sailor stood up and his napkin fell to the bare earth. He was a Norwegian god to some of his customers. A Viking prince to others. A slave girl from Iceland to himself when he was depressed. His tight factory-made shirt was torn in places that made his large chest all the more alluring. "Poor Bailey."

"Let's finish our picnic, boys." Regino wiped his eyes and collected his emotions. "This world is cold. You work and work to build something, and it gets torn away from you. Nothing lasts. Don't ya know that?"

Quiet enveloped the town. The flames had burned so tall that the other buildings had been in danger of catching fire. The Mining Bears had brought their heavy wagons from the river, and with the help of several former Water Mill workers and Babe's Mercantile that supplied hoses, the town was saved.

All except the saloon.

A light wind blew. The sky stretched deep and empty.

"I need walls around me," the sailor muttered.

"Someone's comin'." Poor Montgomery squinted his eyes. "Just one rider, from the old man's ranch."

Regino removed his revolver.

"It's Bold Bullet," Poor Montgomery said. "Put your gun away."

"No." Regino held the gun close to his side.

When the lone rider came within five hundred yards, across from where the saloon had stood, he slowed his horse. "Where can a man get a drink around here?" he asked.

"You can go to hell," Regino shouted. "Murderer. I oughta shoot you right here."

"I protected myself," Andrew said. "That is all I did. I wouldn't try shootin' me. I can't help but hit my mark every time."

"You burned down our business," the sailor exclaimed. "Who'd believe a dandy would destroy the Screaming Lilly!"

Andrew dismounted and led Buchanan the rest of the way to the picnic. "I was only one of many."

"That makes you innocent?" Regino exclaimed. "We're your own kind. They say you love men. I say you're not worthy of the classification."

"I need a drink," Andrew said. "Or some opium. Or both."

"Good luck findin' it," Regino said. "You ain't gettin' any from me."

Poor Montgomery passed Andrew his flask. Andrew nodded in appreciation, uncapped the silver bottle, and took a long draw.

"You're whores just like every other whore I've seen," Andrew said, after wiping his mouth with the back of his tattered blue silk sleeve. "Nothing special about this place. Nothing different from back east."

"No one spits on me here," the sailor said. "No one arrests me here. There's a lot that's different."

"Leave us be," Regino said. "Get away from us, and take your gun and your nail polish with you."

Andrew took another draw from Montgomery's flask, screwed the cap back on, and handed it back.

"I know where you can get some opium," Montgomery said.

Andrew held Regino's cold stare for a moment longer, before leading his horse away with Montgomery.

17. Confrontation at the Blacksmith Salon

"I can't write," protested Christian Joseph St. Martin. He was seated at Olga's desk in the empty schoolhouse. "I don't want to write. I am so angry."

"Anger is a great fuel for work." Olga drew in smoke from his pipe. He rested his feet up on one of the student desks. He leaned his head against the wood planking of the wall and gazed out through the windowpane at the flat empty field outside. "Anger is what brought me to Utopia. Anger is what can create your newspaper. You've got to make up your mind to do the work."

"All I want to write is how Andrew is a liar and a user and everything bad I can think of to say."

"I don't understand you," Olga said. "You looked up to Andrew because he was a gunslinger and a fighter. That's exactly what he did last night. There's nothing different about him except that he –"

"What?"

"Nothing," Olga said. He had decided that it was better not to speak out loud that the boy was angry at being ignored. What good was a hero if he ignored you?

"I don't want to be a newspaperman," the boy said.

"You could write your novel and publish one chapter at a time in your newspaper," Olga advised him. "Once the paper gets started. Did you ever think of that?"

Christian Joseph forgot his anger for a moment. He appeared to be deep in thought. He chewed his pencil and then stopped himself as his father had always used a switch on his hands when he chewed pencils. "All right. One page. First edition. One story. 'BOLD BULLET MURDERS BAILEY YATES LAST NIGHT DURING LILLY INFERNO.'"

Olga's face brightened. "You've got a flare, my boy. I like it. Write it, and I'll get Garrison to illustrate it with a drawing. I know of another printing press. Babe has one stashed in her storage room. We'll put out the *Utopia World* as a weekly."

Christian Joseph didn't appear happy, but he looked more focused. For once, he thought, he was in the middle of one of his stories. He had pointed his finger and accused Andrew of starting the fire so that Bailey later drew his gun. *He had been there*!

He shuddered as it struck him that had he not pointed and accused Andrew perhaps Bailey would still be alive.

Andrew walked with Poor Montgomery toward the Blacksmith Salon. He noticed several of the townspeople peering at him through windows and doorways of the church and from some of the houses on Flume Street.

"They are much afraid of you," Montgomery said. "They know that if they shoot you it will be war with the Wunderfahrts. They know they will lose such a war."

"Why don't they just take the money he offers them and vamoose?" Andrew asked. "Why stay here? What's so special about this place?"

Poor Montgomery shook his head. "You don't understand," and then he shot Andrew a quick curious look. "Or you don't want to understand."

Andrew took a deep breath. The weariness of the evening and of the emotional confrontations of the morning had taken their toll on him.

"You don't even remember me," the willowy whore said. "I thought I'd wait for you to recognize me, and you don't even notice who I am."

The quick and clean air of the morning and the sharp colors of the day did nothing for Andrew's memory. He stopped in front of Babe's Mercantile and looked Montgomery up and down.

Montgomery tried to help jar Andrew's memory. "Monty? From your father's ranch?" Montgomery said. "I even wrote you that I had come out here. I figured you would like it here and that you were like me. Look at you! You are like me! Just twisted up inside."

Andrew stepped back. "I am not at all like you, and I am not twisted up inside. I am no whore. And I'm proud to be a pervert! I shoot people in self-defense. I fight men for sport. I am different, not twisted!"

The right corner of Poor Montgomery's mouth lifted slightly. "That's how you were back on Long Island. You haven't changed. Only now there are many people that want to see you hanged."

"Look, kid, you said you knew where there was some opium."

"Olga Red Bootstragen has it. We're going to the school. She has it buried somewhere."

They walked south toward the schoolhouse.

"We need a sheriff," Monty said. "You could take the job and work for us instead of for the old man."

Andrew was surprised at how funny he found the idea. They had to stop walking while he doubled over with waves of laughter. Eventually, he was able to say, "Me? The sheriff of a town!"

He brushed his long hair back from his face and patted Montgomery on the back to thank him for the laugh. They continued on their way to dig up the opium.

An hour later, they were stretched out on blankets in a back room behind the Blacksmith Salon. The opium had been potent, and Monty had offered some scotch from his flask. He was propped up on one elbow on his side, watching Andrew. Andrew's hands rested behind his head as he stared up at the rafters. "I remember you, Monty. Poor Monty. That's what my father called you. My father the Judge of All That Is."

Monty snorted a short laugh in agreement and passed Andrew the flask. "He used to tell me that I was lucky to work on your farm, that manure shoveling jobs that paid and included meals were hard to find. I used to think that you were stuck up."

"Me?" Andrew took a sip from the flask and turned his head to gaze at the skinny whore. "I was a complete failure. My father paid girls to say they dated me, and he paid a woman to be my wife."

"Landsakes! And you let him?"

"I didn't care. I just took it out on whomever I fought next in the Bowery. I met a lot of men there."

"You didn't think that I was your type?" Monty asked.

"You were too nice." Andrew gave the whore a once-over look. "Although, now that I see you like this, I guess I should have given you more thought."

Montgomery sighed and lay back on the blanket. "I don't think I want you that way anymore. I did when I was a kid. You had all those muscles, and you sure acted like you would do something with me if I wanted, but you ignored me. Now? Well, now you're a killer, aren't you? You killed Bailey. Bailey was my friend. He took me in and gave me a job. You helped set fire to the Lilly, and now I have no place to live. I don't think I want you now, Andrew."

"Why are you here with me then?"

"Curious, I suppose."

They lay there like that for a long time listening to the sounds of hammering coming from the blacksmith's anvil out front. The blacksmith liked oil paintings, and his shop was something of an art gallery, Montgomery had informed Andrew.

At last, Montgomery leaned over and gave Andrew a long kiss. In not too much time they were naked, but only after Montgomery had fastened the latch on the door.

They were awakened by the pounding of the forge. After several minutes the pounding stopped. They heard voices out front. Andrew recognized the loudest one of them as Bastard Ass from the Wunderfahrt Ranch. "We came to pick up our silver horseshoes."

"Leave me be," Petey Schuster, the blacksmith warned.

"We made an order for silver horseshoes last week. Are you telling me you won't fill it?" Bastard Ass said.

"We'll burn your place down just like we burned down the saloon last night," Cancer snarled.

"Not before I shoot you through the eyes," the blacksmith said.

Andrew stepped into his pants and got just one of his suspenders over his bare shoulders. He was aware of Monty getting his shirt on. Andrew jumped onto the floor, unbolted the latch, and gun in hand, he was out into the front room of the Blacksmith Salon. There were indeed paintings everywhere. The walls were covered with brilliant colors, reds and yellows, greens and turquoise.

"Drop your guns, and get out of here now, or I'll send you to hell, you and your sorry friends," Andrew said.

All three of the intruders did as they were told.

Bastard Ass growled. "You work for Wunderfahrt."

"Not anymore," Andrew said. "Get out!"

"Ginger-ass fairy," Bastard Ass muttered. He kicked his horse and turned the reigns. The other men followed him, and they galloped off down Flume Street.

The blacksmith eyed Andrew's bare chest and arms swiftly before extending his hand to shake. His grip was crushing. "I don't know why I'm shaking your hand after what you did last night," he said.

"Don't bother about it." Andrew hitched up his pants, and he and a flabbergasted Monty went into the back room to gather their things.

"You were great back there," Montgomery told Andrew as they left the Blacksmith Salon.

"I don't want your praise," Andrew said. "I hate praise. You can't trust it, and it's always of the wrong kind."

Montgomery shook his head. "You're damaged as they come. Worse. What happened to you back in the big city? Huh?"

"Look, kid," Andrew began. The sun shone high in the sky, and the two men favored the cool shadows of the Blacksmith Salon back overhang. "Don't try to reason me out. I can't even do it myself. I got screwed over by a man, and he's sent bad people after me, so yeah, I don't have a healthy idea of what it means to love men."

Montgomery gestured all around them. "You don't? Here it is, right in front of you. But go ahead, leave us be. Ride out of town like all the men that pay me for love and deny it for themselves. Believe what the opposite sexers tell us, that we're not as good as they are. Forget us, Bold Bullet. We're not worth your trouble."

Montgomery turned his back on Andrew and walked alone to the wood plank walkway of Flume Street.

For several long moments Babe's cold scrutiny made Andrew uncomfortable. "I don't believe men change. I wish I was wrong."

"What if you didn't know what you truly were to begin with?" Andrew said.

A sour frown spread across Babe's face. "There's no one here to make you a sheriff." They sat in her parlor drinking chamomile tea as the afternoon sun sank lower over the hills. "But I've got Randolph's old shirt and badge. All of it. Just like Poor Montgomery told you. Don't know if they'll fit you. Randolph was a bean-pole all right."

"Who pays the sheriff?" Andrew asked.

"The county. They'll have to swear you in. Just formalities. You'll get ten dollars every two weeks."

Andrew thought of his money belt savings. "That will be fine. Give the doctor my best."

"She hasn't come back from the ranch."

Christian Joseph and Garrison clambered up the back steps and rattled about in the kitchen. When at last they entered the parlor, Christian Joseph's face lit up. Just as quickly, the light faded.

The boy cast his gaze downward.

Andrew opened his mouth to speak. He wanted to tell Christian Joseph it was because of him he had turned the corner, that the boy's admiration meant something. Instead, he held his tongue.

"Meet the new sheriff of Utopia," Babe told the boys.

In the Wunderfahrt barn twelve men sat on hay bales and wood benches. The smell of pipe smoke and manure seeped through gaps in the wood and drifted outside into the Wyoming air. "Bold Bullet was the 'special boy' of Senator Hawkins," Mortis told them all. "The Senator doesn't want Bold Bullet to tell anyone of their special friendship. What's more, Bold Bullet killed Goiter's brother. He is our enemy, and he must die."

"Seems easy enough. We just go set fire to him wherever he is. Take maybe an hour," said one of the men.

"No," Mortis said. "Goiter must do it. This is Goiter's last chance."

"Yeah? Beg your pardon, but who exactly are *you*?" another of the men asked. "You come in here and just take over. We take orders from Gretchen Wunderfahrt."

There was an uncomfortable pause before Mortis answered. "I am Mortis. I've killed more men than anyone here."

A heavy silence was followed by murmurs of recognition.

"Are you sure? Micky here killed two families and a scouting party."

"I'm not some sloppy leavings neighborhood thug," Mortis said. "To me, killing is an art."

Goiter blinked. He had always thought of killing as a living not an art.

"We don't have time for 'art,'" another man said. "Gretchen wants us to take over that town by the end of the month. The old man wants those freaks out of the valley."

"I hate them inverts," another man said.

Goiter flinched. All of this waiting around had given him too much time to think. Just why did these men hate the inverts so much? His brother had hated inverts with the same conviction. Goiter had never understood why. The best way to kill someone was to just run right up and do it.

Mortis gave Goiter a hearty pat on the shoulder. "Goiter set fire to the saloon, I hear. He's our champion."

Goiter didn't feel like a champion. He felt stupid sitting there like a good dog on display. He liked working in the shadows instead.

"Doesn't look like a champion to me," Charles said. "Just a city thug with a match is all I figure him for."

Mortis sat up straight and then with a hop, he was on the ground and moved swiftly toward the interloper. He grabbed Charles by his shirt collar and lifted him off his hay bale seat, up into the air so that Charles' feet were off the ground. Charles struggled and clutched at Mortis's fingers locked around his throat. "Goiter is a champion, and I never want to hear otherwise." Mortis shook Charles hard and threw him down upon the ground where Charles lay gasping and coughing. Mortis addressed the others in the barn: "Gretchen wants this done fast, then we'll follow my new plan. We want everyone to know it when Goiter kills the fop."

18. The Sheriff

Walking down the middle of Flume Street came Utopia's new sheriff. The previous sheriff's old clothes made a snug fit, it was true, but Andrew's physique brought new life to the clothing, and the sight was not lost on the boys from the Screaming Lilly.

"He killed Bailey," the sailor reminded everyone. "I don't care how manly he looks in those tight clothes or how many badges he wears, I don't trust him."

Poor Montgomery stopped sweeping the charred remains of tables and chairs into a pile on the open air floorboards of what once was their place of business. "That's Bold Bullet, and if he's our sheriff, you better trust him. He'll save us from the Wunderfahrts."

The sailor spit tobacco into the dirt. "How do you know he's not planted here to help the Wunderfahrts?"

"He's stayin' at Babe's place with the boy. Babe can read malice in anyone. You know that," Poor Montgomery said.

"If that's so," the sailor said, "I wonder how long he'll last?" The sailor kicked a broken beer mug and left Montgomery to sweep up as he sauntered across the rubble. Several large tent sections flapped in the wind sheltering card games of those who could not quit frequenting the sacred earth of the old saloon.

"Wait!" Christian Joseph St. Martin called out.

Andrew turned to face the boy. They stood near the corner of Elephant and Flume. "Is it true? You really are the new sheriff?"

Andrew nodded.

Christian Joseph appeared flummoxed. The hot sun sent kisses of sweat down his forehead. "You're going to protect the town?"

Andrew shrugged. "Can't get out of it now." The right side of his mouth lifted in a wry half-smile. "What's a matter, boy? You look shocked. Get your pencil and write it all down. Didn't I always say I'd be your biggest story?"

A hint of a sparkle entered the boy's eyes. He took several exasperated breaths.

"I'm done struttin' around town in these tourniquet clothes. Let's go back to Babe's and figure out what we're going to do."

Christian Joseph took a step back.

"What's the matter?"

The sparkle was gone. Horror took its place. Bailey would not have died if Christian Joseph hadn't pointed his finger at Andrew that night. The boy was sure of it. And if it weren't for Andrew, there would have been no reason to point his finger! Christian Joseph turned on his heels and ran all the way home without ever looking back.

"We're going to take the town Saturday morning," Mortis said. "And that's when you'll kill the Nancy."

They stood watching the ranch hands lasso a calf. Since the ranch hands were mostly thugs, the lasso-ing was a sloppy drawn-out affair.

Dust rose from the large pen. "The whole town will witness what you do," Mortis went on. "There'll be proof for the gang back in the Five Points you fulfilled your mission."

Goiter nodded in agreement although he really didn't understand.

"Politics is a slimy snake." Mortis took a drink from a flask in his coat pocket and carefully replaced it when he was through. His red stringy hair hung from beneath a dark black cowboy hat. "The Nancy claims he was with Senator Hawkins like man and woman. The Nancy attended that invert party back in New York. Got arrested. Picture was on the front page of the paper. If the Senator's name gets mentioned–"

"Why hasn't he mentioned it yet?" Goiter asked.

"Maybe he's just running away." Mortis turned to face Goiter, away from the moronic attempts at lassoing. "Or maybe they aren't lies. Who knows? All I know is the Senator runs that gang and what he wants he gets. You blew your chance, and I'm here to give you another."

The intensity in Mortis' face frightened Goiter. It didn't make sense. Mortis wasn't the type who helped people. He wanted Goiter to do the dirty work, plain and simple, and he wanted Goiter to take the blame. Mortis would have clean hands. Maybe the trick to being a successful assassin was to have other people do the dirty work for you. Probably it was the trick to staying alive altogether.

"Thank you," Goiter lied.

Gretchen Wunderfahrt wrung her hands together. Her father refused to approve of anything she did, and now she was forced to guard a captive Black doctor for sale to Kansas bounty hunters.

Dr. Gray sat cross-legged on the floor of the storm basement with her hands tied behind her back. She could see the light diminishing from the high windows at ground level above. "Your father knows I am the only doctor for miles. How will getting rid of me help him?"

Gretchen clutched her stomach. "He also knows there is nothing that can be done. He probably searched your bag for laudanum for himself. Now he intends to use you as a bargaining chip to take over the town."

Dr. Gray winced with frustration. She thought of her friends back in Utopia, of Christian Joseph and Babe, of the days and weeks she had spent fighting to get to Utopia from Ohio.

"And you agree with him?" the doctor asked.

"This valley is ours. Has been for one hundred years. Your... *people* ... have no right to it. Least of all a Black woman."

The doctor clenched her jaw. "We women have no right to any-thing."

Gretchen ceased her pacing. She looked the doctor over as if for the first time. "No."

"Untie me then."

Gretchen felt her face grow hot.

The doctor looked her directly in the eye. "Yes. You do understand what I mean. You do what your father tells you. He expected the same of me. He owns people, and in particular, women. The two of us, we deserve better than that. We run our own lives."

"Shutup!" Gretchen shouted. She made an awkward short rush at where the doctor was seated on the floor and waved her arms. "You're a—!"

"—free woman. More than you can say."

Gretchen felt her brain might explode. She wanted to do violence to this brazen prisoner, and yet just as much, the doctor spoke the truth for her.

"Inside of you must be the same as it is for me," the doctor continued. "You want the chance to break out and take what is yours, beholden to no man, once and for all. The world is run by men, but it shouldn't be, and we both know that."

Gretchen felt surprise as tears began forming in her eyes. "Men!" cried Gretchen. "They own everything. They control everyone. They seduce women, and they seduce each other. They are weak, vain, shallow, childish, cruel, and pompous asses.

"I am so alone!" Gretchen announced. She turned her back resolutely to the staircase, away from Dr. Gray. Slowly, she climbed the steps and closed the door behind her, leaving the doctor alone with a rapidly thudding heartbeat, in the dark of the basement.

Andrew stared after the runaway child for several moments before taking his first step to follow him. As he passed the Blacksmith Salon, a voice from the shadows hissed, "You killed Bailey!" and two heavy men jumped him from behind. Their weight bent his back, and he fell to the ground with a painful thud. He groaned as their fists pummeled him on his chest and stomach. He tried to shield his face. "Hold him down!" a gruff voice shouted, and a heavy boot kicked him hard in the side, over and over. "This is for Bailey."

Andrew tried to crawl away, to kick in defense, but the blows kept coming and then blackness engulfed him.

"I'm not a doctor," Babe said as she bent over Andrew and finished adhering a fresh bandage to his stomach. He was badly bruised. He tried to raise himself up on his elbows, but the pain paralyzed him.

"You fought back the Angel of Death," Garrison proclaimed. He was dressed all in black with a white sash over his left shoulder. His breath smelled of chocolate.

"Go do your homework," Babe commanded him.

"No! Bold Bullet is my hero! He's our new sheriff. He's the only one around here with the guts to put on that outfit and stand up for all of us. I know what it's like to be beaten up. The boys at school hated me ever since I performed all the parts of *Troilus and Cressida* at the sow breeding festival."

"You rest," Babe told Andrew. "Dr. Gray is gone seeing a patient, but when she gets back –"

"She can't stand him any more than the rest of the town," Christian Joseph hissed from the shadows in the back of the room.

"I thought you were working on your newspaper," Babe said.

"I am," Christian Joseph said. "I'm sketching our sheriff on his sickbed for the front page. Our brave sheriff."

Garrison practically flew across the room, his sash sailing off behind him. "Give me that!" He tore the pad of paper away from Christian Joseph. "How dare you sketch him like that!"

The boys tumbled across the wood floor as Babe screamed and tried to separate them. When at last she did, Christian Joseph sat up. His shirt was uncharacteristically disheveled. "This man isn't some character from one of your little plays. He uses people."

Garrison leaned in close to Christian Joseph. "Nobody likes him just like nobody likes me. He's my idol!"

Christian Joseph threw down his pad and left the room.

Garrison sank down to the floor and stretched out his legs. He covered his face with his hands. "Nobody knows better than me what it's like to be a pariah, to be hated in your own land."

"Oh, God," said Babe as she cleared away the medical supply kit.

"To be misunderstood. To be a creative artist stuffed with talent at such a young age."

Later in the afternoon, Garrison returned to give Andrew a bouquet of prairie flowers arranged tastefully with grass flourishes and an unexpected cornhusk to provide a conversation starter.

Andrew winced as Babe propped his head up on pillows. "Thank you, boy. And indeed, I am quite honored you intend to write a play about my life."

Christian Joseph watched from the sick room's doorway. He folded his arms.

They were all seated around Andrew's bed the next day.

"I heard all of the ranch hands are coming into town on Saturday," said Poor Montgomery. "Heard it from my number one client. He knows one of them. They plan to take us over and chase us out."

"Oh my Lord!" Garrison grabbed his head and writhed about.

"Enough," Babe whispered to him.

Garrison brightened. "We could meet them with you."

Andrew patted the boy's shoulder. "You need to stay alive to write this all down in your play. I probably need some deputies."

"This town has never unified for anything," Babe said. "You weren't at our town meeting."

"I'll do it," said Poor Montgomery.

"A whore? As a deputy?" Babe exclaimed.

Christian Joseph felt himself bristle. How dare that little frontier drama queen, Garrison, let Andrew pat him on the shoulder. If anyone should be patted on the shoulder, it was Christian Joseph! He waited until everyone had left the room and Babe closed the door to let Andrew rest.

"Just who do you think you are?" he said as Garrison passed him in the hallway.

"A gifted *theatrique*. I'm about to write a play about the first sheriff of my kind. I'll be famous, at last!" Garrison took the end of his white sash and tossed it around his neck with a flourish.

"Stay away from him unless you want to eat that scarf."

"I'm not afraid of a pasty boy from Ohio," Garrison retorted at slightly too high a volume. "We'll just see who is Bold Bullet's friend."

Christian Joseph felt short of breath. Babe would be mad at him if he cut Garrison into tiny little bits. And besides, wasn't he through with Andrew? He felt dismay that apparently he was not.

The week passed and still Dr. Gray had not come home.

Maybe she doesn't want to return because I am living at her house, Andrew thought. *She hates me that much now.*

Andrew stood outside watching Olga Red Bootstragen and Babe hacking at an ancient stump to clear it from the garden. He carried a shovel to where they were toiling and commenced to dig around the base of the huge obstruction.

"Even in pain, he picks up a shovel to help," Garrison mewed from the back porch where he stood watching next to Christian Joseph. Garrison wore a turban fully twelve inches high, fashioned from a colorful horse-blanket. "He's so handsome and stylish. I want to be just like him."

"You'll never be just like him," Christian Joseph said. "He can't stand artifice. I traveled across the country with him. I got to know how he thinks."

"Yes, but he's commissioned me to write a play about him."

"You pretentious little foof!" Christian Joseph gave Garrison a hard shove.

"You've dislocated my shoulder!" Garrison shouted. He felt for his turban, found it had fallen into a puddle of pig slop, geared himself for a mad dash like a Pamplona bull, and launched himself at Christian Joseph.

"Stop them!" shouted Babe. "I won't have fighting on my property!"

Andrew put down his shovel and hurried to where the two boys were rolling in the dirt. Babe had them both by their collars and shook them hard. "Enough!"

"Believe me." Andrew winced and held his side. "Fighting never got me anywhere."

Christian Joseph avoided Andrew's eyes. Instead he saw riders and horses on the horizon.

"Get inside," Babe told the boys. When neither of them moved she shouted, "Now!"

Andrew checked for his gun. He motioned for Babe to follow the boys.

"This is my store." Babe remained at Andrew's side.

Six riders approached and came to a stop. In the center of the ring they formed with their horses around the garden sat Goiter and Mortis. The two men advanced to the railing of the back porch, but they did not dismount.

"Did you run away from the ranch?" Goiter asked. "Like a chicken?" The right side of his mouth lifted slightly.

"Heard a rumor they made you sheriff," Mortis said. "Makes sense for a dandy town."

"I volunteered," Andrew said.

"Why?" Goiter asked. "Cowards can't be sheriffs."

"No, they can't," Andrew said. "Where is Dr. Gray?"

"Old Man Wunderfahrt is sick," Mortis said. "I heard she's stayin' with him till he gets better."

Andrew stared at Goiter until Goiter looked away.

"Why don't you come back with us now and save everyone a lot of trouble?" Mortis said.

"So the gang sent you to finish what Goiter couldn't do?"

Mortis looked off into the distance as he spoke. "We want to call a meeting with you, *Sheriff*. The Wunderfahrts want their town back. No need for people to get hurt or ... killed." He spat tobacco at the base of the steps.

Babe bristled and opened her mouth in protest but thought better of it.

Mortis observed the faces of Christian Joseph and Garrison peering at him through the back window.

"When do you want this meeting?" Andrew asked.

"Saturday morning. Say 11?" Mortis answered. "Here at the store."

"No. We'll meet at the church," Andrew said.

Mortis spat again, clicked his tongue, pulled the reigns, and led Goiter and the other four riders back to the ranch.

Christian Joseph watched through the window as Andrew and Babe walked slowly back to the boulder arm and arm. "You wanted drama, well now you got it."

"All those men from the ranch are going to invade our town on Saturday," Garrison said quietly. "People are going to get hurt."

"Isn't that the drama you like?"

When Garrison didn't answer, Christian Joseph realized it was the excitement he thought he had ached for ever since he had left his home in Quincy. He watched Andrew speaking with Babe. "We have to help him," Christian Joseph told Garrison.

"I thought you didn't like him."

"People change."

Garrison chewed his lower lip and then stopped himself. "I have an idea."

19. Secret Meeting

Torches burned around the entrance to the Bear Mine. Gorgeous Fenster, Genius Ward, Olga Red Bootstragen, Poor Montgomery, Babe, and Andrew sat around a table in the lounge.

"Fenster, you and Genius lead the bears to the ranch along with Babe and anyone you can gather. There'll be no protection there Saturday morning. Dr. Gray is in trouble. It's our best chance," Olga said.

"The old man is going to sell her to the traders," Genius said. "He threatened to do that to me more than once. He wanted my opium for free. He's forcing her to doctor him for free, to stay there to keep her freedom."

"Ain't gonna happen," Babe said.

Andrew turned to Olga Red Bootstragen and said, "It's up to us to organize everyone who's left to bring their guns and take places along Flume Street and around the church: Petey Schuster and the women at the Blacksmith Salon and their families. Those ranch hands think we won't fight."

Olga played with the hem on his red skirt. "You killed Bailey. You're no friend to Utopia."

"So the Wunderfahrts can just ride in and take the whole town away from you?" Andrew said.

"There'll be those that will defend the town, but not those who will defend you."

The others stared at Andrew, waiting for his response.

Fenster cleared his throat. "He's got the guts to wear that little sheriff's outfit like a sideshow target, means he's all right by me. I'll leave some of the bears to help you."

"They don't have to," Andrew said. "I can do my own defending. They just need to be near the church, at the dentist's and at the Mercantile Store on the lookout."

After the meeting, Poor Montgomery offered Andrew a bit of loco weed and a swig of corn whiskey out by Andrew's horse.

"Imagine you have so much power that you can send a hired killer into the wild west to execute your ex-boyfriend. The same boyfriend you once held in your arms and whispered you loved more than anyone else in the world." Andrew took a sip of whiskey and tilted his head back to look at the sparkling stars. "You're a senator with heavy ties to a Tammany Hall Gang who does your dirty work for you. You are paranoid the ex-boyfriend might tell a newspaper what you really are." Andrew handed Poor Montgomery the bottle. "And all those dainty twisted men with their careers and their secret parties and secret signals married to wives they don't love, and the rough trade who beat out their self-hatred in fights and assaults. That's the world we left behind, Monty."

Poor Montgomery took a hit of weed from his pipe. "You'll love again, Andrew."

"You can't love if you're dead."

20. Nothing More

Saturday morning broke bright and crisp. Dr. Gray dipped a green cloth into a basin of hot water. She was giving Old Man Wunderfahrt a sloshy sponge bath. "Where are all the ranch hands going?" she asked when she saw them gallop off together from the window.

"They're going to destroy your invert village," Old Man Wunderfahrt answered.

Dr. Gray squeezed the sponge harder than necessary.

"Those people won't fight, but if they do, my men are cut tough. Besides, I have a secret weapon."

Dr. Gray soaped the flaccid skin of the old man's upper right arm.

"Here woman! Gently!" he exclaimed.

She asked him what the weapon was.

The old man licked his thin lips. "Turn away while I wash myself!" he commanded her.

Dr. Gray decided there was a God after all. "Certainly."

Several plops and sloshes later the old man said, "The Sheriff. He works for me."

"Andrew?"

"Bold Bullet is his name. I told him to get all those inverts to trust him and then let my boys take over. Towel."

Dr. Gray wiped her eyes on her sleeve.

"Towel! Good God, woman, are you crying? Gretchen! Come here and take this crying Black away."

Gretchen hurried inside the kitchen as Dr. Gray stood up. Gretchen grabbed for her arm, and the doctor pushed her back. "I don't believe it," Dr. Gray said.

"Hey!" the old man called and then gurgled.

As the doctor fended off another grab attempt by Gretchen her eyes widened at the sight of the twitching naked old man in the tub. "He's having an attack!"

"Daddy!" Gretchen rushed to the tub.

Dr. Gray pushed her aside. "Give him room."

"What can we do?" Gretchen pleaded.

"We'll get him out of the tub and into bed. That's all we can do."

They wrapped the shaking pallid man in towels and Gretchen held him close. "Daddy?" To Dr. Gray she cried, "He doesn't answer me."

Dr. Gray let Gretchen carry her father to a settee in the parlor off the kitchen. She covered him in blankets and tried to give him a glass of water, but the old man wouldn't drink. Gretchen knelt next to the settee, and when she looked up to ask Dr. Gray wasn't there anything else that could be done, she found the doctor pointing a pistol from Gretchen's very own riding bag left open by the door, at her chest.

"Help him!" Gretchen pleaded.

"There's nothing I can do. His heart is weak. I'm going to walk out of this house and take one of your horses and go help my friends."

A solitary tear ran down Gretchen's cheek. "It's not that simple."

21. Reasoning With The Enemy

Breakfast that morning had been solemn. Garrison was dressed all in black. Christian Joseph ate his favorite grits, greens, and biscuit combo. Babe spoke nary a word. Andrew sat at the head of the table and downed two cups of strong coffee. He wore his sheriff's outfit and star.

Poor Montgomery poked his head in the open doorway from the little rose-lined lane outside.

"Not used to seeing you in long-sleeves," Babe said. "You're transformed."

Monty grinned timidly. "It's almost nine. I'll walk you to the church."

Andrew wiped his mouth with a napkin. "You boys swear you'll stay here?" he asked Garrison again.

Christian Joseph pretended not to hear.

Andrew sighed. "Kid, even if you hadn't pointed your finger at me, Bailey would have seen me and tried to shoot me. It would have happened the same way without you. It's not your fault."

Christian Joseph swallowed the last of his biscuit and looked up at Andrew. "I can't get my mind around it."

Andrew gave Christian Joseph a searching look. "You're talking to me again."

"I was *always* talking to you!" Garrison blurted.

"I wanted adventure, but I didn't understand," Christian Joseph said.

"It hasn't been that long, but something is grown up about you now, boy," Andrew said. "Cynicism has been added to your ingredients."

Christian Joseph was about to open his mouth and argue that that wasn't the case, but Poor Montgomery interrupted. "Let's go, Sheriff."

Down the middle of Flume Street in the main part of town, Andrew and Poor Montgomery walked alone toward the church. The sun beat warm upon them with a cool breeze of autumn.

Around them as they walked, in the shops, the Blacksmith Salon, and even the House of Nude Dentistry, Andrew heard doors and windows open and shut. He witnessed a bear from the mines dart behind the jailhouse. He watched faces peer timidly out from behind drapes and shutters. He heard rifles cock and spied gun barrels at the ready, but only a handful, behind woodpiles and around corners.

Far off at the end of the road at the other side of town from Utopia Church, Andrew noticed perhaps twenty men on horses waiting.

"That doesn't look good," Monty said. "Too many of 'em."

Andrew remembered what they taught him at the Little Gentlemen's Academy, to walk away when outnumbered. He smiled inwardly. He wasn't a little gentleman anymore.

Not a human sound was to be heard in Utopia that moment. Only the call of one faraway watchdog barking endlessly at the vast prairie.

"Wait out here." Andrew put his hand on Monty's chest to stop him.

"But –"

"Wait here."

Andrew entered the church alone.

22. Fight For Life!

Bastard Ass and Cancer stood guard outside the Wunderfahrt ranch house. This Dr. Gray learned when from behind her Bastard Ass ordered her to drop her gun.

"You are gold to my father!" Gretchen cried. "And you do nothing?"

"His heart has failed. There is no treatment for that."

"Oh Daddy! It's your little Gretchen. I'm here. I've got you!" Gretchen cradled the old man's wizened head in her lap. She had pulled him to her from his pillow on the bed.

"I said drop your gun," Bastard Ass warned Dr. Gray.

The Mexican War bubbled in the doctor's memory along with a technique she had learned from a flour burglar in a raid. She dropped her pistol on the floor. As it clacked and skidded she punched her right leg backwards behind her into the kneecap of Bastard Ass. He cried out and fell forward. He fired once into the floor as he fell. She grabbed his arm and snatched his gun, before kicking him in the stomach.

"Get up!" Dr. Gray yelled at Gretchen.

"Go ahead and kill me," the other woman answered. "You'll never be anything more than what you are – a white man's tool."

Over the moaning from Bastard Ass on the floor, Dr. Gray heard the clomping of heavy boots on the stairs outside. Holding a gun in each hand she waited for the door to open.

The worst part of anxiety was trying to disguise it from those around you. Goiter had tried to appear rock steady as he waited seated atop his horse at the end of Flume Street. His legs trembled, and his balance in the saddle felt questionable. He dismounted and figured standing next to his horse on solid ground would steady him, but his legs would hear nothing of it and the trembling continued. Mortis and Andrew had been too long talking inside Utopia Church. The only hope was that they would come to an agreement and the town could be taken over peacefully. All Goiter would have to do would be take Andrew back to the ranch and shoot him in the head in front of Mortis as a witness.

What seemed a simple killing gnawed at Goiter.

The moments waiting became endless. He didn't like that the skinny whore called "Monty" stood posted as a sentry outside the church's front door. The town remained utterly peaceful. A crisp autumn morning. Sun on damp wood. Jays squawking on the roof. Goiter heard the odd rustling behind window curtains and doorways. No one walked along the boardwalks. They must all know that this morning was the big morning.

Goiter felt a chill. If the townspeople knew about the meeting, wouldn't they try to defend their town?

Inside the church, Mortis waited in the shadow of the altar.

"Hello, Ralph," Andrew said. "Or should I not call you that?"

Mortis snorted once and stepped out into the speckled light from the one stained-glass windowpane high above them. "Don't matter what you call me, accountant."

"Sheriff now."

"Let's stop wasting time," Mortis said. "If you don't surrender, I can't be responsible for what happens to you or the town. It's out of my control."

"Yes, you always did have other people do your dirty work. Back in the Five Points when you sent Goiter's brother after me, you think I don't know it was you working for the Senator?"

"Pretty smart for a poof," Mortis said. "I heard the rumors about you and Senator Hawkins. But the Senator had his hands in the gang. He even said he hated poofs, too. And you with that so-called wife of yours, that woman from the orphanage, we all heard your father paid her to live with you."

"She didn't suffer. She ran that house. She was tougher than some of you."

Mortis gave Andrew an appraising look.

"Get off of me and my kind," warned Andrew.

"You're out here," Mortis said. "And who knows what you'll say especially now that you're wearing that sorry excuse for a badge."

"New York is two thousand miles from here. Who cares what I say?"

A scaly smile spread across Mortis' face. "The Senator cares. Stories travel. But dead poofs can't spread rumors. Surrender the town, and I'll let you go."

Andrew chuckled. "You always were a lizard, Ralph. Let me guess. If you secure the town for old Wunderfahrt, you earn a huge bonus. Then, when you let me go you have Goiter shoot me in the back. Goiter does it to save his life and avenge his brother. Goiter possibly hangs for my murder. Your hands, as always, remain clean. The Senator, as always, gets what he wants, the maintenance of his phony image and the complete betrayal of the only thing that was true in his life. Me."

"What do you care about this town?" Mortis countered. "You pretend to stand up for them. You never took a stand in your life."

"You think you know me from the gang," Andrew said.

"We'll see."

Goiter jumped with a start when the gun crack sounded from inside the church. He scrambled back up into his saddle, fumbled with the reigns, kicked the sides of his horse and cried out "Yeehaw!" something he had learned on the ranch. The other ranch hands did as he did.

Christian Joseph held Garrison's arm even after the boy's gun fired into the church ceiling.

Andrew and Mortis swung their heads toward the back pew. Mortis drew a pistol and aimed it.

"They're just boys!" Andrew lunged at Mortis and knocked him to the floor before the gun went off.

"Let me fire again!" Garrison pleaded to Christian Joseph.

"Too late," Christian said as he watched Mortis scramble to his feet and flee out the back door.

Christian Joseph snatched Garrison's gun. Garrison squirmed and freed himself from Christian's grip and then ran out the front entryway to the street.

Christian Joseph turned once again to face the altar. "Bold Bullet!" But Andrew had followed Mortis out the back.

Christian's heart beat heavily. He would never catch them if he followed Mortis and Andrew. He figured he could intercept them through the alleyways if he left through the front.

Outside he saw Goiter's gang at the far end of the street spur their horses.

Activity blossomed all around him, at Babe's Mercantile, the Blacksmith Salon, and Olga's schoolhouse.

At the House of Nude Dentistry, Josh Breeze wore a holster around his waist, a round of ammunition over his shoulder, and nothing else. Bent over his patient, the sailor from the Screaming Lilly (who the rules of the House allowed could be clothed but who chose to remove his shirt anyway because he liked not wearing a shirt), Josh pulled the last of three lower teeth that candy and chewing tobacco had rotted away. "Chew on this." Josh handed the sailor several cocoa plant leaves when he was through, "...you won't feel any pain. And grab your shotgun and help me with this trouble."

At the Blacksmith Salon, Petey Schuster and his workers hurled iron mallets at the charging ranch hands. And at Babe's Mercantile, Christian thought he saw meat cleavers being waved by a gang of the remaining Water Mill women charging into the street.

But it was the sight of Olga Red Bootstragen standing in the alcove of the upper window of the schoolhouse silhouetted by the American flag flapping in the wind behind him. He held his rifle up in the air as a call to arms. "Utopia, fight for life!" he shouted. "Fight for life!"

Christian felt a warmth in his chest and a smile come to his lips before he noticed through the windows below two ranch hands mounting the stairs to the window alcove.

"Oh no," he whispered. He rushed across the street, careful to duck the in-flight weaponry and dodging the horses of the charging ranch hands. In vain, his eyes searched for the white sheriff's outfit of Bold Bullet.

When he couldn't find it, he raced ahead to the schoolhouse.

Goiter's worry became alarm. The ranch hands attacked the town in reckless disorder. Mortis was nowhere to be seen, nor Andrew. Up above him, townspeople fired upon the invaders. A woman in a red dress perched atop the schoolhouse roof shot a rifle into the air.

He spurred his horse in a gallop through the town through clouds of dust toward the church to find Mortis and Andrew.

When he reached the church, shots were fired from the top window. The skinny whore glared down at him. "If you want Bold Bullet, you'll have to get through me first!"

Two ranch hands leapt upon the skinny man, and Montgomery's bullet missed and hit the dirt near Goiter's horse with a *thuck*.

Behind him, a woman ran by in a torn dress, screaming. Goiter smelt burnt wood in the wind. His horse reared its head, and he lacked the skills to control it. The horse threw him, and he landed in the dirt on his right side. The air left his lungs all at once, and he gasped as the panic around him increased. He covered his head with his hands before resolve returned to him. He clambered to his feet and ran behind the church to find Bold Bullet.

Christian Joseph never had excelled at running, but he made it inside the schoolhouse in record time. Garrison's gun felt heavy in his hand. He took the stairs two at a time and found the two men in the attic tearing at Olga's dress. He shot the man closest in the leg. The other took a bullet in short order. When they were both dead Olga stared at him in amazement. Christian ran to him, and Olga took Christian into his arms. Olga smelled of the booze of the men.

Outside they heard Babe shrieking, "Garrison!" At the attic window they could see the street down below.

In the street, Babe shivered and hugged herself. Garrison struggled to escape, but Mortis held him fast with a gun to his head. Andrew burst out from behind the dentist's office and, at the sight of Garrison in a hostage situation, stopped stock-still.

"We claim Utopia for the Wunderfahrts or the boy dies."

"Let him go! The town already belongs to the people of Utopia!" Andrew shouted.

"An invert lady-man who ran away from New York telling lies about a politician. That's what you people got wearing your sheriff's costume. Surrender yourself to my men right now, Sheriff, and we'll take the town with no bloodshed."

Goiter found his way to the crowd facing Mortis and Garrison. He and Mortis made eye contact with a slight nod. "Give yourself up to my man, Goiter," Mortis called to Andrew.

"Anything happens to that child, and this town won't stop until every last one of you lost cowboys is dead. You know that. If I'm such a poof, why are you afraid to step out from behind that boy and fight me like a man?" Andrew tossed his gun in the dirt and motioned for Mortis to do the same.

Mortis signaled to Goiter to join him. He handed Garrison to Goiter who cupped the boy's mouth and held his arms. Mortis motioned for his men to stay put and ordered them not to fire. He turned back to Andrew and said, "So a poof thinks he can fight like a man?" He threw his own gun to the ground.

"I saw you in New York," Andrew said. He rolled up his sleeves. "At a party only poofs attend."

Mortis's face flushed red. "Another lie." He removed his jacket and tossed it to one of his men.

They advanced toward each other.

I can do this, Andrew thought.

Shouts and cheers erupted from the crowd on both sides.

From the sidelines, Christian Joseph swallowed hard.

The men put up their fists and crouched low to the ground, maneuvering back and forth.

Mortis scooped a handful of dirt and threw it in Andrew's face. Andrew ducked but not in time. The dirt blinded him, and Mortis hit him low and plowed him backward onto the ground.

Olga held Christian Joseph back.

The men rolled, and Poor Montgomery saw the flash of brass knuckles on Mortis's hand. Several others saw the sight, too, and exchanged worried glances.

Andrew turned on his side and kicked Mortis's legs out from under him in a tactic well known in the Five Points.

They both regained their feet. The look in Mortis' eyes grew cold and snakelike. He rubbed his fists through his black gloves and advanced toward Andrew.

"Get that dandy!" shouted the ranch hands.

"Fight him, Bold Bullet!" shouted Monty and several of the townsfolk.

Andrew crouched, lunged, and activated the Little Gentleman's Jiu Jitsu of the East combined with dirty street-fight flourishes. The townspeople broke into cheers and whistles.

Mortis was swift. He evaded several punches and bait-and-switched Andrew with his own that culminated in one hard sharp connect to Andrew's right ear.

Andrew stumbled backward several steps. The ranch hands applauded and catcalled. Andrew raced back at Mortis. In a flying lunge he grabbed the larger man's shoulders and head-butted him. Mortis collapsed.

The town cheered. Andrew quickly regained his footing, found Garrison and Goiter in the crowd, tore Garrison from Goiter's stunned grasp and pushed the boy toward Babe's waiting arms.

The town cheered some more. Before Andrew could turn back to the fallen Mortis, Mortis had swiped him with a thick arm, grabbed Andrew by the leg and pulled him down. They rolled and wrestled around the corner of the dentist's office into a tight alley.

Andrew straddled Mortis and pulled his arm back to deliver a shattering blow to the face. The sound of the gun barrel being cocked not several feet behind him stopped the fighting men and quieted the crowd.

Goiter stood above them.

"Kill him!" Mortis groaned.

Goiter's face filled with angry tension.

"Kill him here!" Mortis yelled.

Goiter fired his gun. There were screams from the crowd as the bullet sound popped. Christian Joseph loudest of all.

Andrew roared. Mortis's blood sprayed across his shirt. Andrew rolled onto his elbows away from the dead man and looked up at Goiter and the gun barrel trained on Andrew's face.

Goiter was impressed Andrew didn't blink. He remembered his twin brother begging and pleading for mercy in fights. The fights started mostly because Goiter's twin had instigated them. Mortis was like Goiter's twin in that way. They were men that never helped anyone.

Goiter lowered his gun and raised his chin.

"Don't shoot!" Andrew shouted at Monty and Babe and several of the townspeople and ranch hands as they pushed their way into the narrow space.

Andrew and Goiter watched each other a moment. Goiter nodded slightly at Andrew. He crouched and leapt from the steps to the side alley beside the church. He ran the length of a building, found his untied horse, and rode off.

"You can't keep this town." Stritch stood before the remaining ranch hands.

"We can't?" Andrew grimaced as he rose to his feet and brushed off his white pant legs. "Look!" He pointed to the hills. The site of the Wunderfahrt Ranch in flames beyond the far end of the alley inspired a collective gasp from those that saw it.

---

23. Nobody's Hero

Dr. Gray closed her eyes and then made a face as she tried to inhale fresh air. The smell of smoke lingered through the open window of Babe's Mercantile. The doctor could see the ruins of the Wunderfahrt Ranch at the far end of the valley, charred broken frames of wood against the brown of the Utopia Hills.

She stroked the smooth skin beneath her lips. At last the irritation from fourteen years of spirit glue and phony beards had healed.

She read again the telegraph from Andrew's lawyer father in New York in response to Monty's letter. The missing surveyor records had been located after an extensive search and several payoffs in Kansas City and verified. The Wunderfahrt Ranch did not encompass the entire valley of Utopia or the land of the town proper. Wunderfahrt had not filed the correct papers with the federal government and had only assumed possession of the remaining valley citing manifest destiny and something not in the books referred to as: Wunderfahrt's law.

She turned around to find Poor Montgomery fresh from being sworn in as the new mayor and a man she recognized from the dance who had fancied Andrew. They stood talking in low tones where Andrew sat with a fresh bandage wrapped around his ribs and a white patch over his eye. She hadn't seen Andrew laugh unguardedly like that and the sight made her happy.

So did Andrew's announcement to the town that the stolen cash box from the stagecoach had been returned. He had worked out a deal with a Kansas City marshall who happened to be a regular at the Screaming Lilly.

All that remained of the old Andrew was the black fingernail paint and the eyeliner he wore.

Old Man Wunderfahrt had told her Andrew would betray the town, and she had refused to believe it, but it could have gone either way. She wished she were a better judge of men and women, but she had found they were utterly unpredictable.

Placed on the tall chest of drawers near the window was the burnt torch she had used to light the Wunderfahrt Ranch House aflame. She had carried it all the way back when the Bears escorted her home. It was an ugly memento, and one she hadn't planned to keep. She wondered if perhaps she had simply been in a state of shock at her own actions. She had beat back the two ranch hands who had found her with Gretchen. She shot Cancer and kept Bastard Ass hostage. Gretchen hadn't hindered her, much to her surprise. In fact, when her father was pronounced dead from a heart attack, Gretchen had come back to Utopia with her.

Oh, not in any romantic way. God, no. More as a compatriot. There she sat, having coffee with Babe at the small eating table. Since the Ranch House had burned, Gretchen seemed light of heart and giddy at the turn of events.

Truth was, so was Dr. Gray. She almost could not remember her real name or Andrew's. Names could be shed like identities, she had learned.

"I heard what you did to save Utopia." A pretty woman dressed in purple stood near the order desk. "You burned down the Wunderfahrt Mansion."

"It wasn't my intention."

"I'm Willa Ward, Genius Ward's sister. I've been wanting to meet you."

Dr. Gray nodded in affirmation. She shook the young woman's hand. She let her eyes linger. The young woman appeared not to mind.

To manage her surprise, she turned back again toward the open window. Outside Garrison reenacted for a crowd of school children the entire "Battle for Utopia," in which of course, Garrison was the star. She watched him pantomime the thick arm of the evil Mortis, where it clutched him around the neck as he was held hostage.

"Bold Bullet!" she heard behind her. Christian Joseph dashed through the store's entrance.

"Look!" He shoved a sketch pad into Andrew's hands.

"What is it, boy? You are a man of constant chores and duties these days."

"First issue of my newspaper," Christian Joseph announced proudly for the entire room to hear.

The cowboy and Poor Montgomery gathered round behind Andrew. "Utopia Saved!"

"That's just the news story," Christian St. Joseph explained. "I want to profile Bold Bullet. I plan to–"

"You keep up your writing. You'll go far." Andrew grabbed his hat from the rack and gave the cowboy a pat on the shoulder. "But don't write about me."

"Why? You're our sheriff. The sheriff of Utopia!"

Andrew shrugged and opened the door. "I'm just a man like any other." He untied Buchanan and tipped his hat to them as he mounted his horse and rode off toward the center of town.

Christian Joseph stood in the doorway.

"Never you mind about him," the doctor soothed the boy. "We've got a town to build."

About the Author

In addition to writing fiction in many forms, Mike has founded two comedy groups, has produced for television and film, and continues to perform standup and improv comedy despite warnings from the authorities.

He lives in Los Angeles.

Sign up for his free newsletter and find out more about his work at www.MikePlayer.net